I can identify colors.

You need:

Color the red.

red

Trace the word **red**.

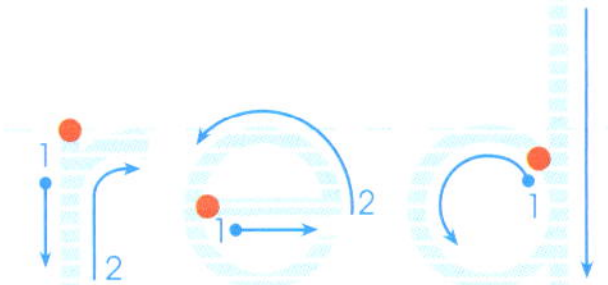

Use your **red** crayon to color the ladybugs.

Got it! OK Not yet

I can identify colors.

Color the orange.

Trace the word **orange**.

Use your **orange** crayon to color the pumpkins.

Got it! OK Not yet

I can identify colors.

You need:

Color the banana yellow.

yellow

Trace the word yellow.

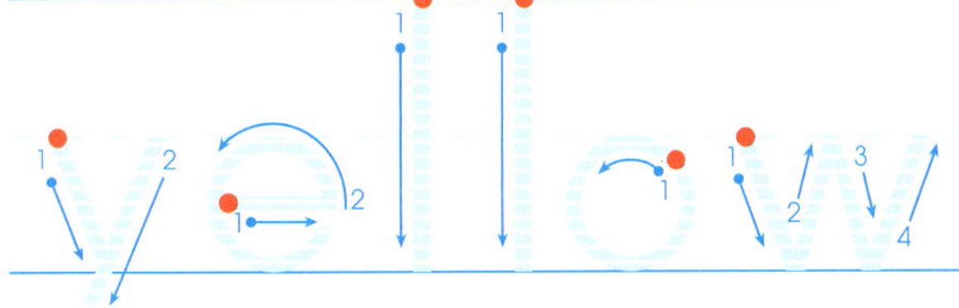

Use your yellow crayon to color the bus.

Got it! OK Not yet

I can identify colors.

Color the green.

green

Trace the word **green**.

green

Use your **green** crayon to color the trees.

Got it! OK Not yet

I can identify colors.

You need:

Color the blue.

blue

Trace the word blue.

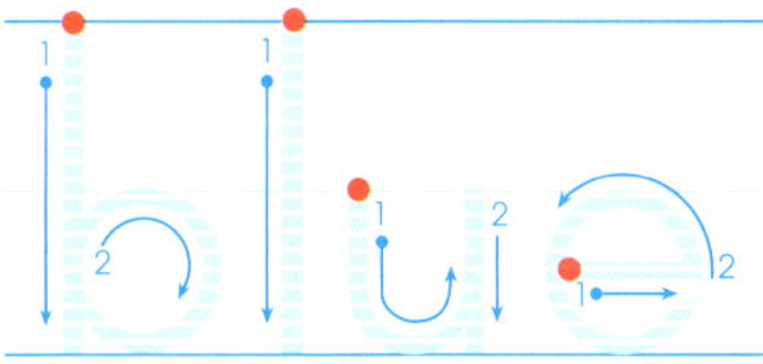

blue

Use your **blue** crayon to color the eggs.

Got it! OK Not yet

I can identify colors.

You need:

Color the purple.

purple

Trace the word **purple**.

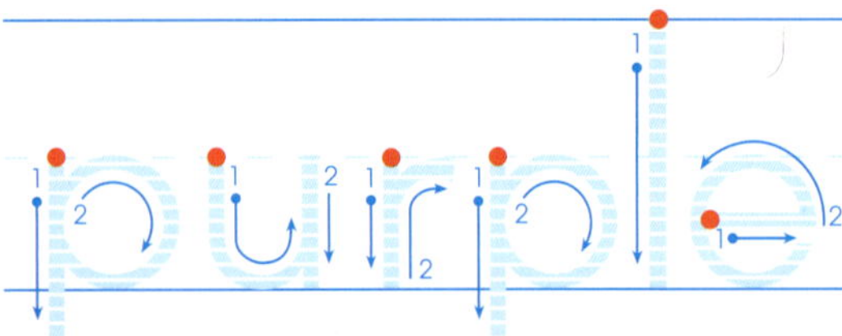

Use your **purple** crayon to color the grapes.

Got it! OK Not yet

You need:

I can identify colors.

Color the flamingo pink.

Trace the word pink.

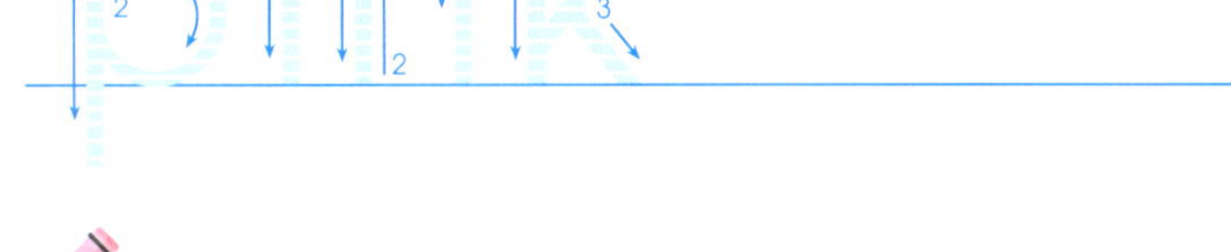

Use your pink crayon to color the cake.

Got it! OK Not yet

I can identify colors.

You need:

Color the squirrel brown.

brown

Trace the word **brown**.

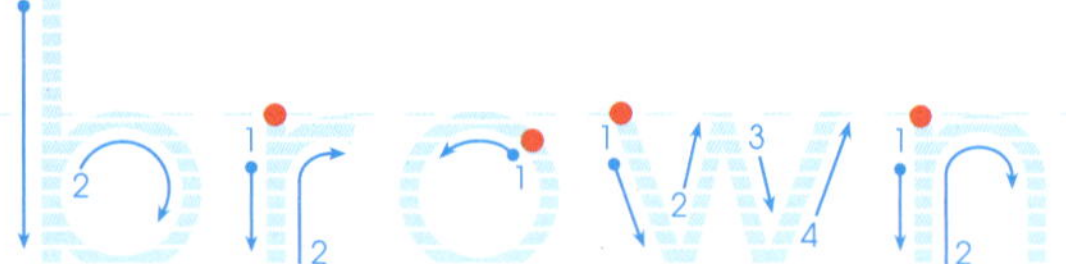

Use your **brown** crayon to color the log.

Got it! OK Not yet

I can identify colors.

Color the koala gray.

Trace the word **gray**.

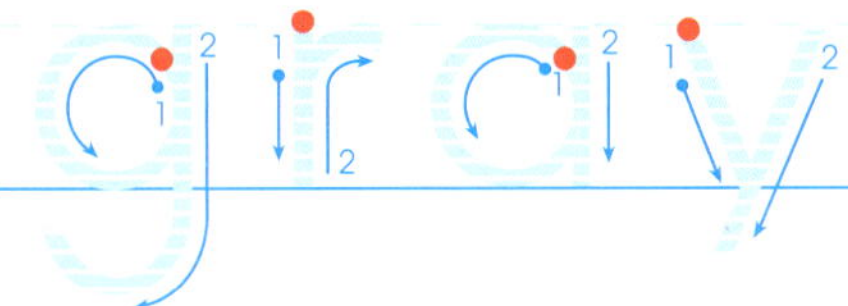

Use your **gray** crayon to color the whale.

Got it! OK Not yet

I can identify colors.

You need:

Color the cat **black**.

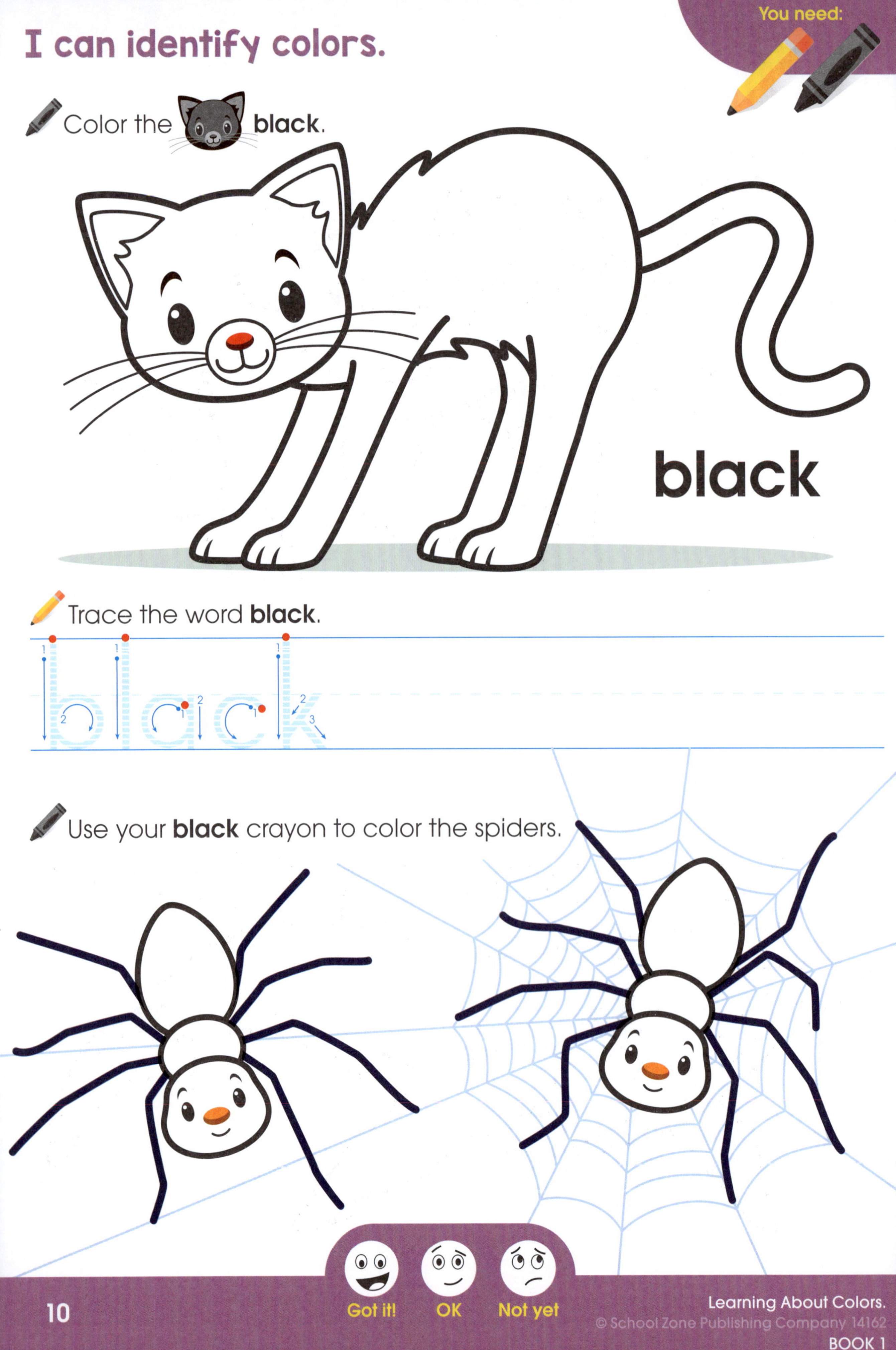

Trace the word **black**.

Use your **black** crayon to color the spiders.

Got it! OK Not yet

I can identify colors.

Trace the word white.

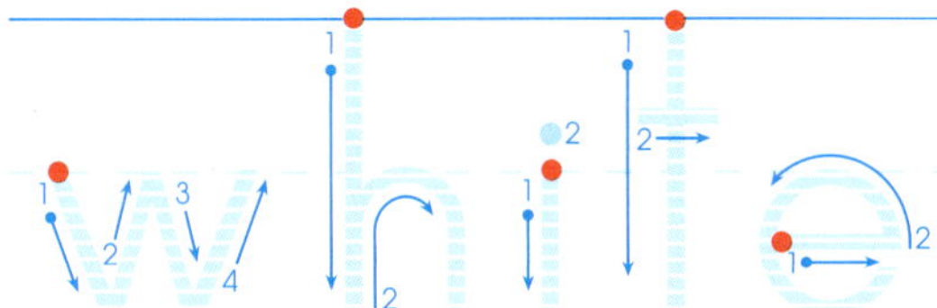

Circle all of the things that are usually white.

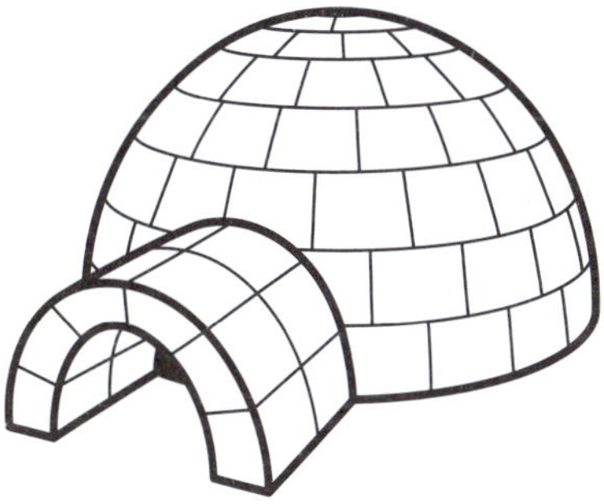

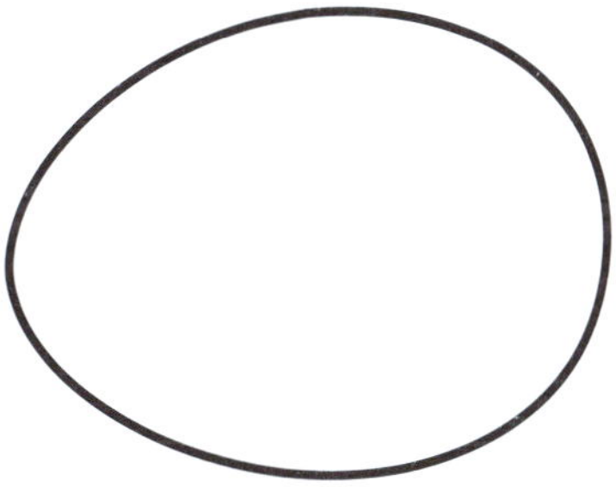

Got it! OK Not yet

Let's have some fun!

Color the scene.

1 = green   2 = red   3 = blue   4 = orange   5 = brown

Got it!   OK   Not yet

You need:

I can read and understand kindergarten books.

Cut out the booklet pages below and fold along the center line. Combine these pages with the booklet pages from page 15 to make a book. Then read the book out loud.

MY HATS

By C. B. Hatt

Fold along this line.

MY HATS

BLUE

RED

GREEN

PINK

WHITE

I like my green hat.

I like my red hat.

I can read and understand kindergarten books.

Cut out the booklet pages below and fold along the center line. Combine these pages with the booklet pages from page 13 to make a book. Then read the book out loud.

I like my pink hat.

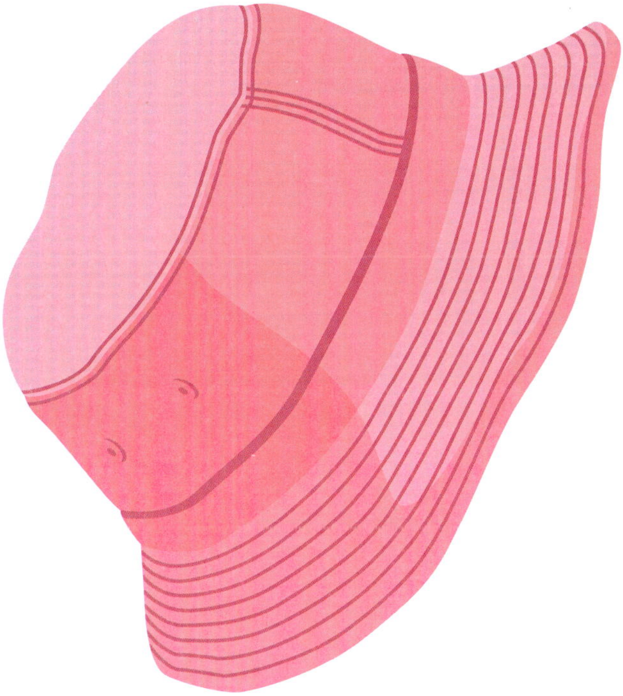

Fold along this line.

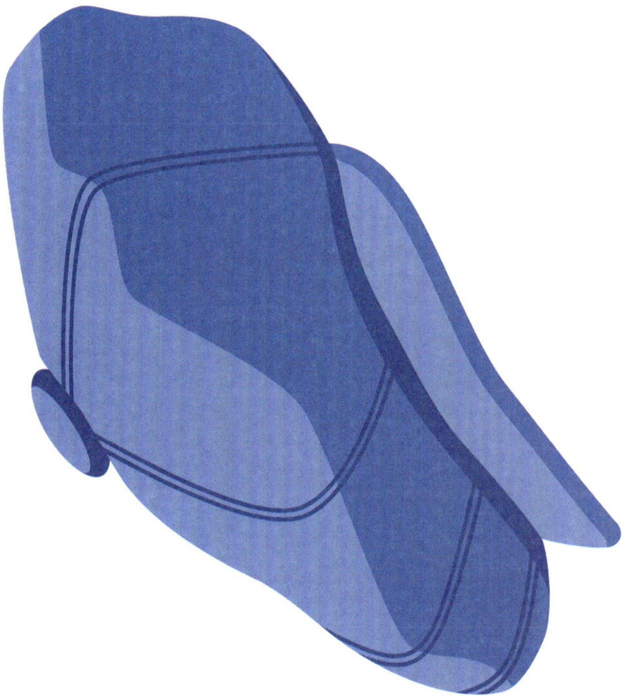

I like my blue hat.

Color the hat below in your favorite color.

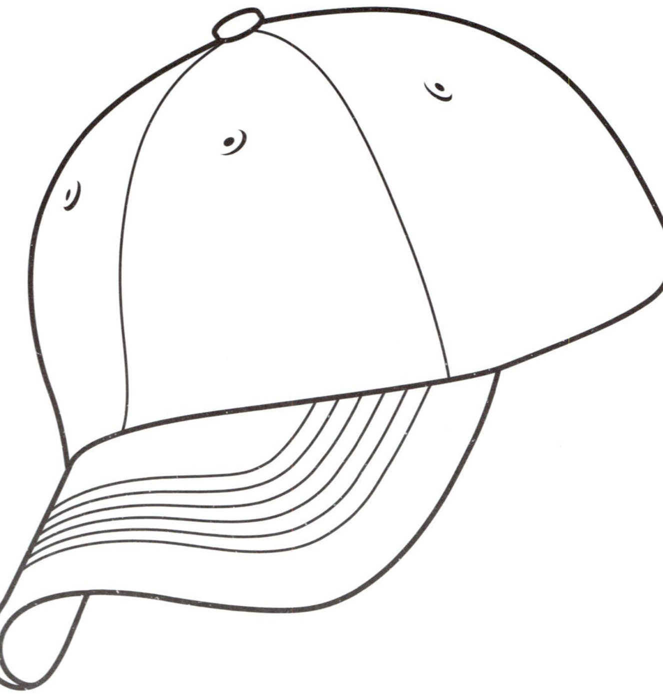

Write the color you made the hat.

I LOVE my

hat.

I can recognize all uppercase and lowercase letters in the alphabet.

Trace and write the letters.
Start at the red dot (●).

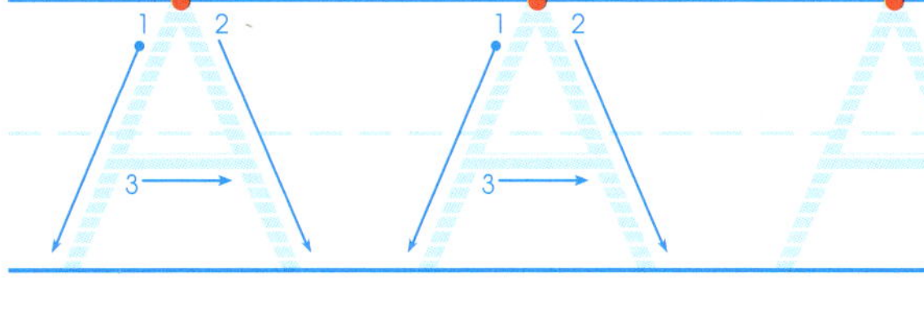

Color the picture.

Trace the letters to finish the sentence. Start at the red dots (●).

A is for astronaut.

Got it! OK Not yet

I can recognize all uppercase and lowercase letters in the alphabet.

Trace and write the letters.
Start at the red dot (●).

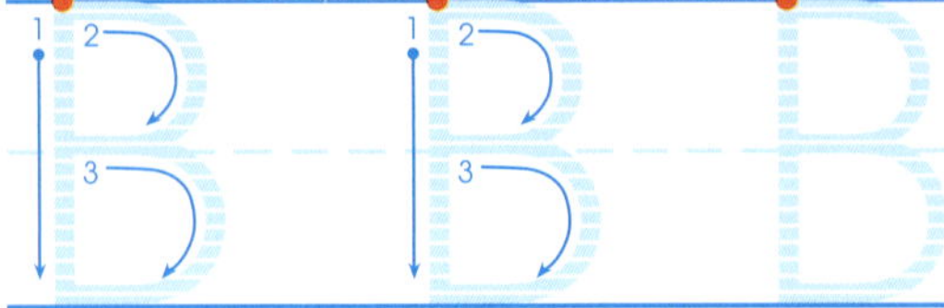

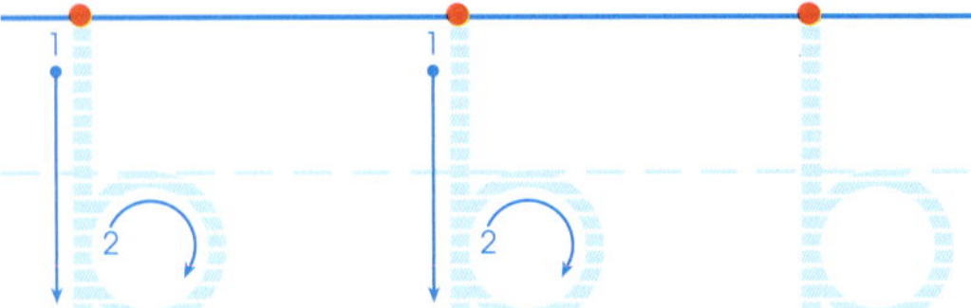

Color the picture.

Trace the letters to finish the sentence. Start at the red dots (●).

B is for bee.

Got it! OK Not yet

CCSS.ELA-Literacy.RF.K.1.D

I can recognize all uppercase and lowercase letters in the alphabet.

Trace and write the letters.
Start at the red dot (•).

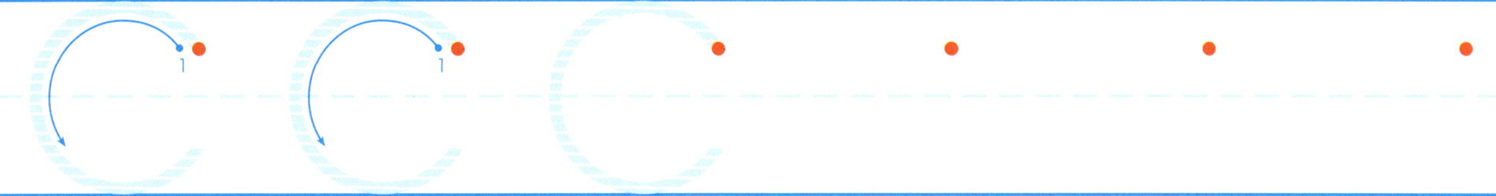

Color the picture.

Trace the letters to finish the sentence. Start at the red dots (•).

C is for cat.

I can recognize all uppercase and lowercase letters in the alphabet.

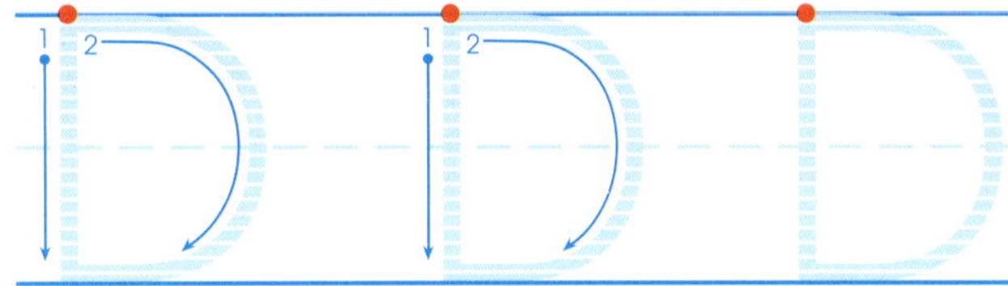

Trace and write the letters.
Start at the red dot (●).

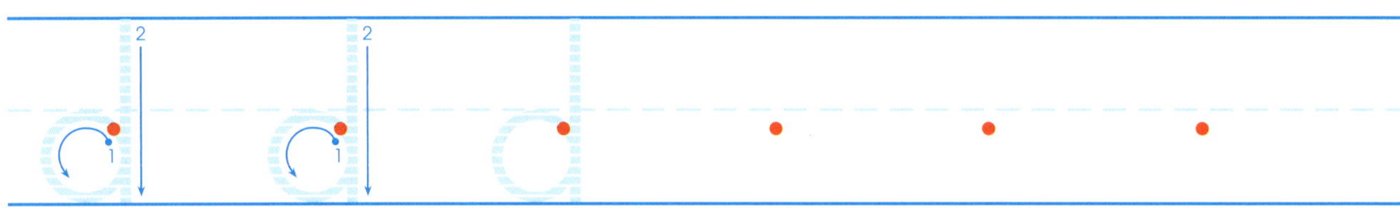

Color the picture.

Trace the letters to finish the sentence. Start at the red dots (●).

CCSS.ELA-Literacy.RF.K.1.D

I can recognize all uppercase and lowercase letters in the alphabet.

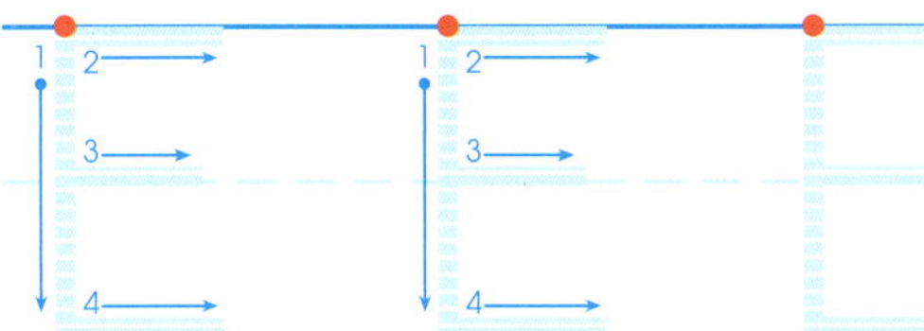

Trace and write the letters.
Start at the red dot (●).

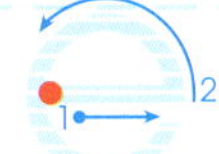
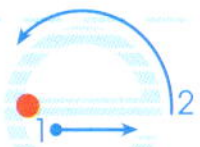

Color the picture.

Trace the letters to finish the sentence. Start at the red dots (●).

E is for elk.

Got it! OK Not yet

I can recognize all uppercase and lowercase letters in the alphabet.

Trace and write the letters.
Start at the red dot (●).

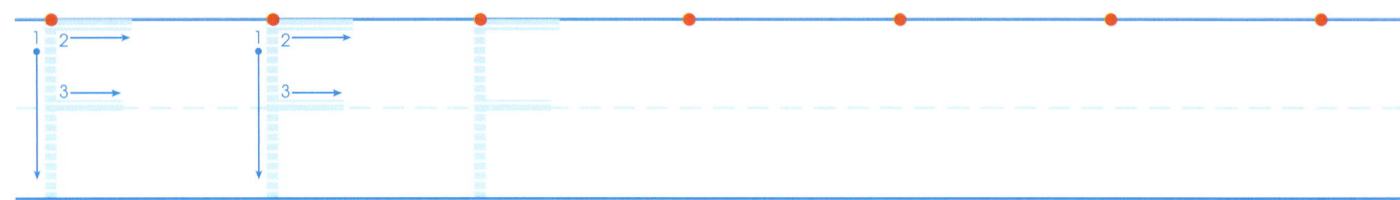

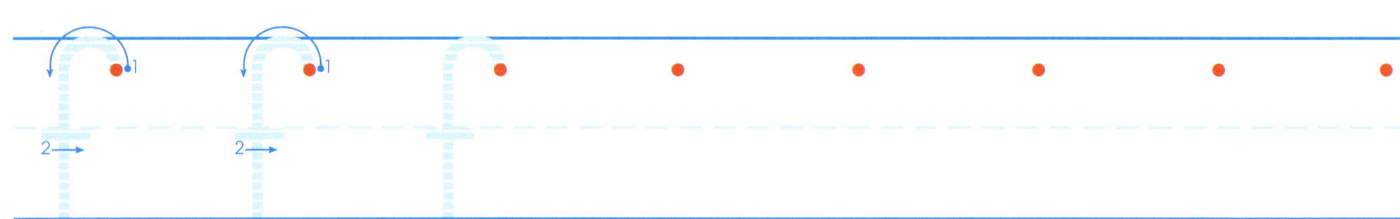

Color the picture.

Trace the letters to finish the sentence. Start at the red dots (●).

F is for frog.

CCSS.ELA-Literacy.RF.K.1.D

I can recognize all uppercase and lowercase letters in the alphabet.

Trace and write the letters.
Start at the red dot (●).

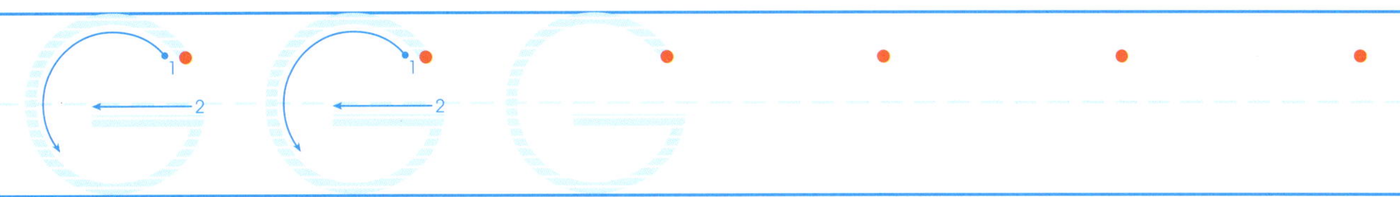

Color the picture.

Trace the letters to finish the sentence. Start at the red dots (●).

G is for goat.

You need:

I can recognize all uppercase and lowercase letters in the alphabet.

Say the name of each picture.
Underline the letters in each row that begin the name of the picture.

E f F L f

a d A V a

C o a C c

R b P B b

b d D a D

Got it!

OK

Not yet

CCSS.ELA-Literacy.RF.K.1.D

I can recognize all uppercase and lowercase letters in the alphabet.

Draw a line from each uppercase letter to the matching lowercase letter.

A	c
B	d
C	a
D	b
E	f
F	g
G	e

Got it! OK Not yet

I can recognize all uppercase and lowercase letters in the alphabet.

Trace and write the letters.
Start at the red dot (●).

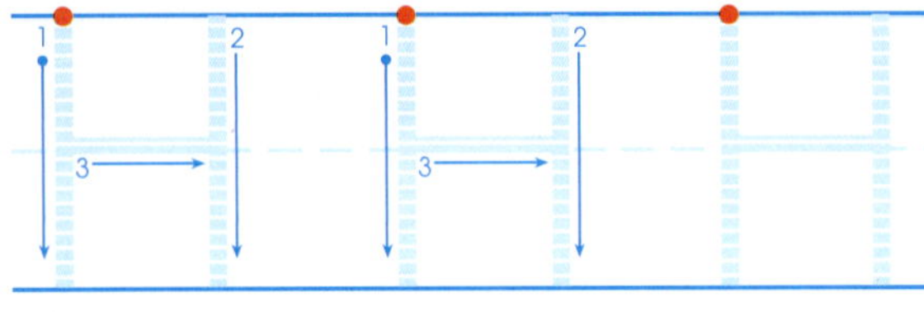

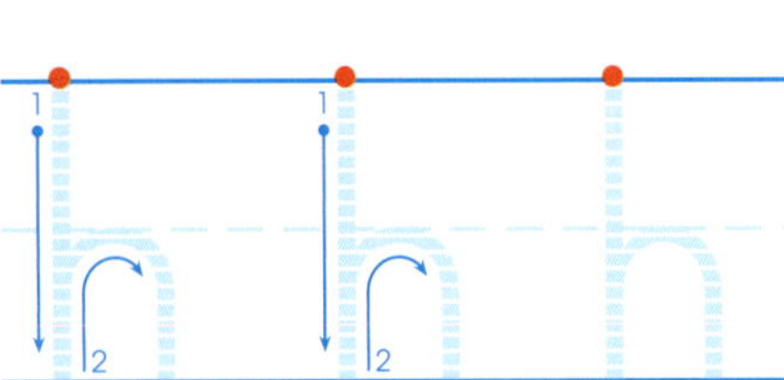

Color the picture.

Trace the letters to finish the sentence. Start at the red dots (●).

H is for hamster.

Got it! OK Not yet

CCSS.ELA-Literacy.RF.K.1.D

I can recognize all uppercase and lowercase letters in the alphabet.

Trace and write the letters.
Start at the red dot (●).

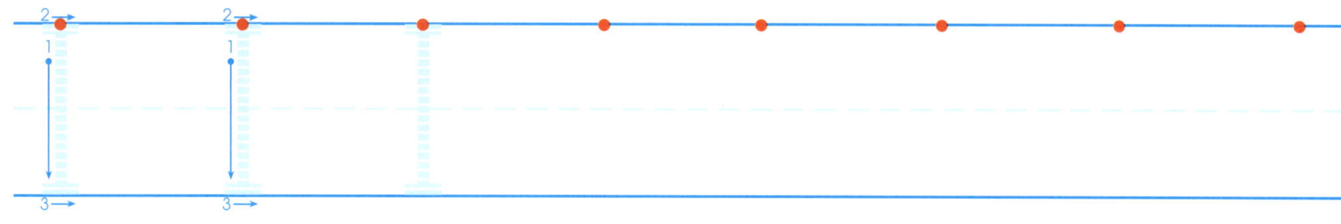

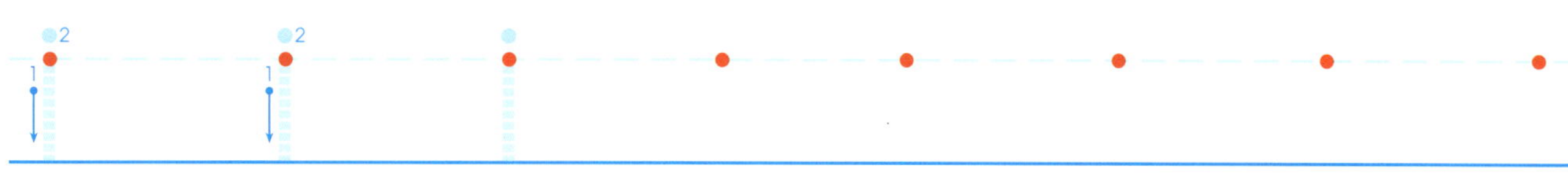

Color the picture.

Trace the letters to finish the sentence. Start at the red dots (●).

I is for iguana.

I can recognize all uppercase and lowercase letters in the alphabet.

Trace and write the letters.
Start at the red dot (●).

J J J

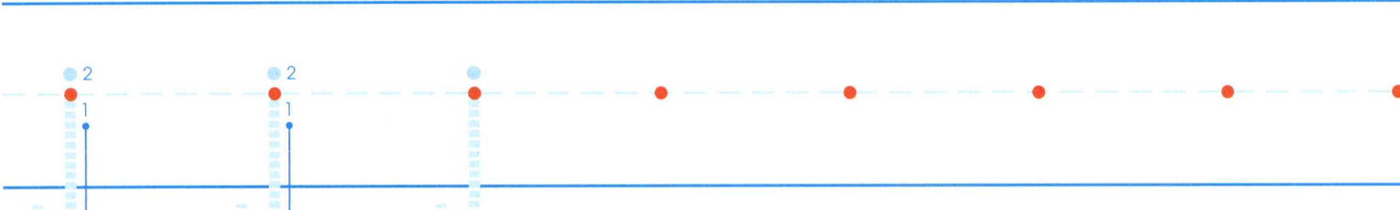

Color the picture.

Trace the letters to finish the sentence. Start at the red dots (●).

J is for jet.

I can recognize all uppercase and lowercase letters in the alphabet.

Trace and write the letters.
Start at the red dot (●).

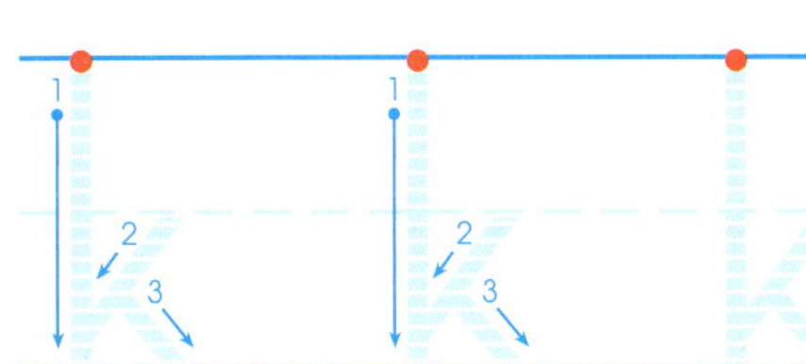

Color the picture.

Trace the letters to finish the sentence. Start at the red dots (●).

K is for kite.

Not yet

I can recognize all uppercase and lowercase letters in the alphabet.

Trace and write the letters.
Start at the red dot (●).

L L L

l l l

Color the picture.

Trace the letters to finish the sentence. Start at the red dots (●).

L is for lion.

CCSS.ELA-Literacy.RF.K.1.D

I can recognize all uppercase and lowercase letters in the alphabet.

Trace and write the letters.
Start at the red dot (●).

M M M

m m m

Color the picture.

Trace the letters to finish the sentence. Start at the red dots (●).

M is for monkey.

I can recognize all uppercase and lowercase letters in the alphabet.

Trace and write the letters.
Start at the red dot (●).

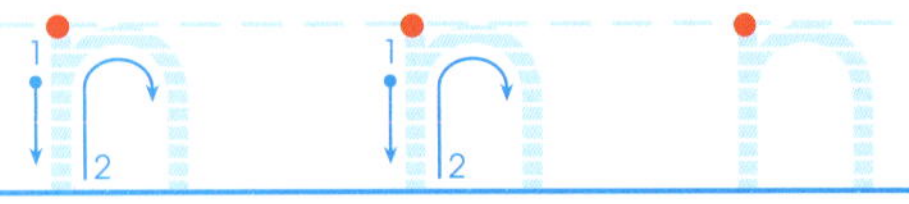

Color the picture.

Trace the letters to finish the sentence. Start at the red dots (●).

N is for nest.

CCSS.ELA-Literacy.RF.K.1.D

I can recognize all uppercase and lowercase letters in the alphabet.

Connect the dots from **A** to **L**.
Color the picture.

You need:

I can recognize all uppercase and lowercase letters in the alphabet.

Say the name of each picture.
Underline the letters in each row that begin the name of the picture.

G g b G C

h b H E h

U j J g J

I i T i L

L i l I D

Got it! OK Not yet

CCSS.ELA-Literacy.RF.K.1.D

I can recognize all uppercase and lowercase letters in the alphabet.

Draw a line from each uppercase letter to the matching lowercase letter.

H	i
I	j
J	h
K	k
L	m
M	n
N	l

Got it! OK Not yet

I can recognize all uppercase and lowercase letters in the alphabet.

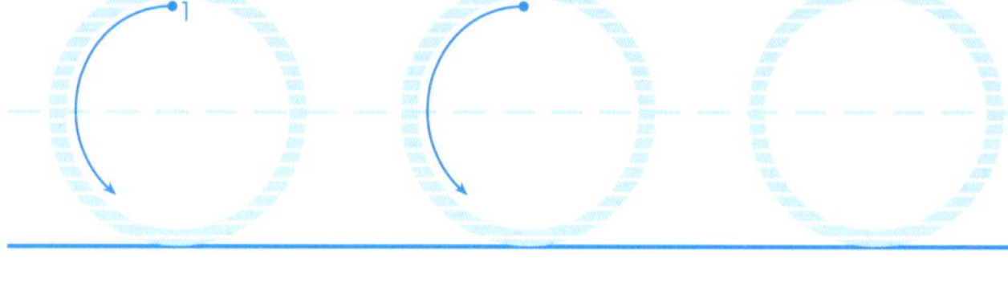

Color the picture.

Trace the letters to finish the sentence. Start at the red dots (●).

is for tter.

Got it! OK Not yet

CCSS.ELA-Literacy.RF.K.1.D

I can recognize all uppercase and lowercase letters in the alphabet.

Trace and write the letters.
Start at the red dot (●).

P P P

p p p

Color the picture.

Trace the letters to finish the sentence. Start at the red dots (●).

P is for penguin.

Got it! OK Not yet

I can recognize all uppercase and lowercase letters in the alphabet.

Trace and write the letters.
Start at the red dot (●).

Q Q Q

q q q

Color the picture.

Trace the letters to finish the sentence. Start at the red dots (●).

Q is for quail.

Got it! OK Not yet

CCSS.ELA-Literacy.RF.K.1.D

I can recognize all uppercase and lowercase letters in the alphabet.

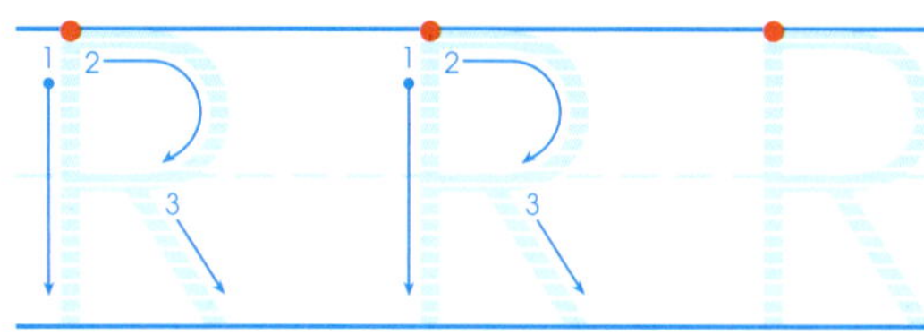

R R R

Color the picture.

Trace the letters to finish the sentence. Start at the red dots (●).

R is for robot.

Got it! OK Not yet

I can recognize all uppercase and lowercase letters in the alphabet.

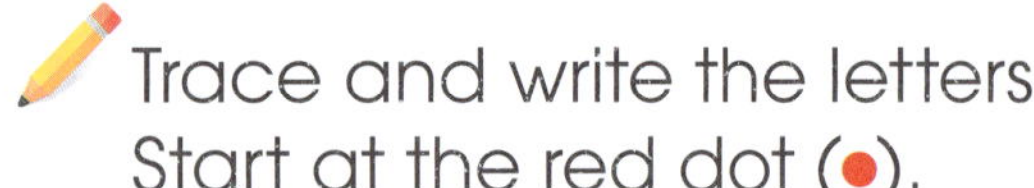

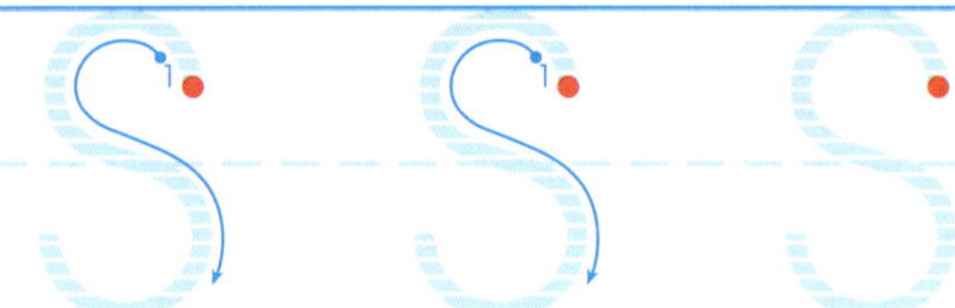

Trace and write the letters.
Start at the red dot (●).

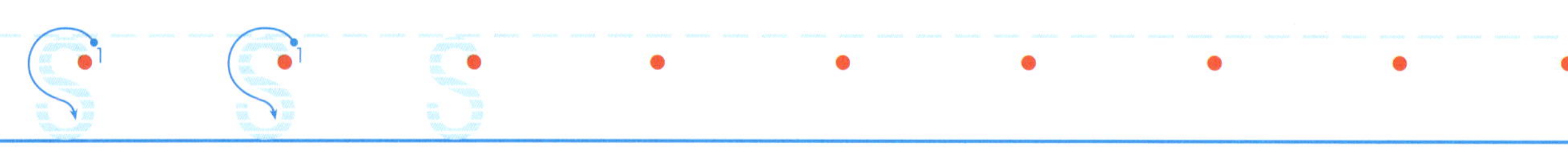

Color the picture.

Trace the letters to finish the sentence. Start at the red dots (●).

CCSS.ELA-Literacy.RF.K.1.D

I can recognize all uppercase and lowercase letters in the alphabet.

Trace and write the letters.
Start at the red dot (●).

Color the picture.

Trace the letters to finish the sentence. Start at the red dots (●).

is for iger.

Got it! OK Not yet

I can recognize all uppercase and lowercase letters in the alphabet.

Connect the dots from **A** to **R**.
Color the picture.

D F O M E C H N K G L P B A I J R Q

Got it! OK Not yet

CCSS.ELA-Literacy.RF.K.1.D

I can recognize all uppercase and lowercase letters in the alphabet.

Say the name of each picture.
Underline the letters in each row that begin the name of the picture.

P D p b P

o O C Q o

m N V n N

q Q o Q C

R n r P r

Got it!

OK

Not yet

I can recognize all uppercase and lowercase letters in the alphabet.

Draw a line from each uppercase letter to the matching lowercase letter.

O	p
P	q
Q	o
R	t
S	r
T	s

Got it! OK Not yet

CCSS.ELA-Literacy.RF.K.1.D

I can recognize all uppercase and lowercase letters in the alphabet.

Trace and write the letters.
Start at the red dot (●).

U U U

u u u

Color the picture.

Trace the letters to finish the sentence. Start at the red dots (●).

U is for umbrella.

I can recognize all uppercase and lowercase letters in the alphabet.

Trace and write the letters.
Start at the red dot (●).

V V V

v v v

Color the picture.

Trace the letters to finish the sentence. Start at the red dots (●).

V is for violin.

Got it! OK Not yet

CCSS.ELA-Literacy.RF.K.1.D

I can recognize all uppercase and lowercase letters in the alphabet.

Trace and write the letters.
Start at the red dot (●).

W W W

w w w

Color the picture.

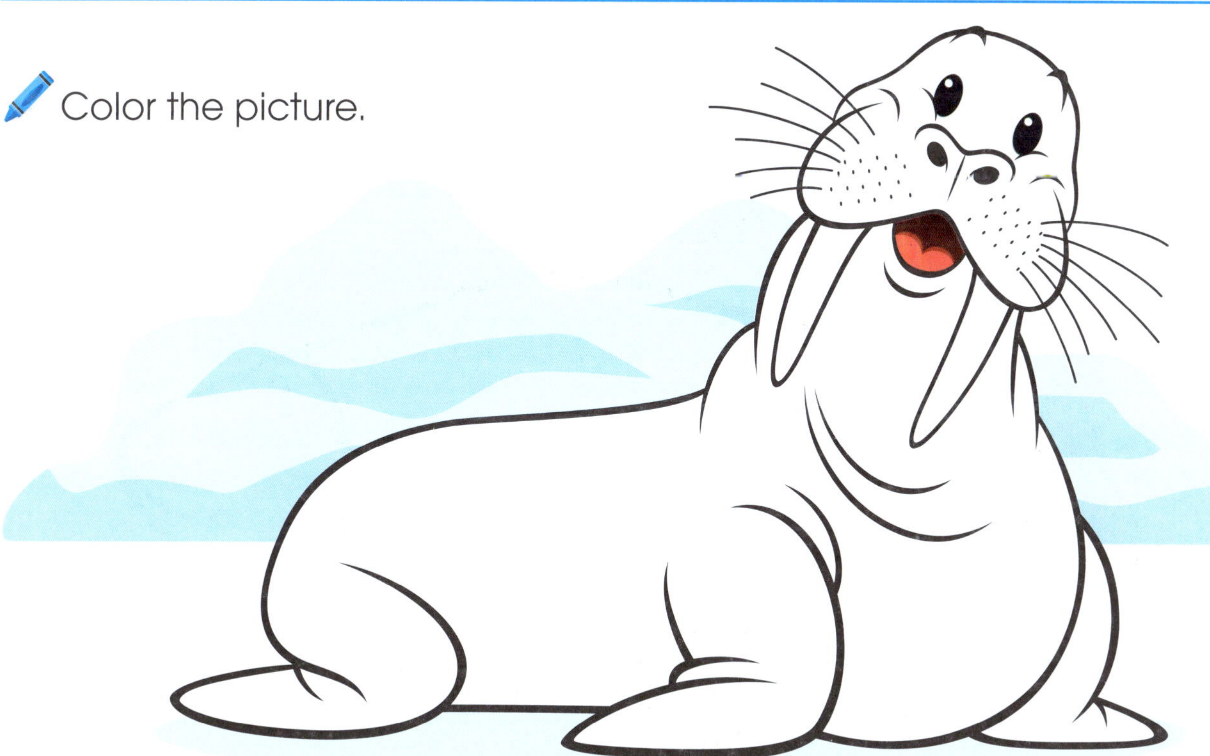

Trace the letters to finish the sentence. Start at the red dots (●).

W is for walrus.

Got it! OK Not yet

I can recognize all uppercase and lowercase letters in the alphabet.

Trace and write the letters.
Start at the red dot (●).

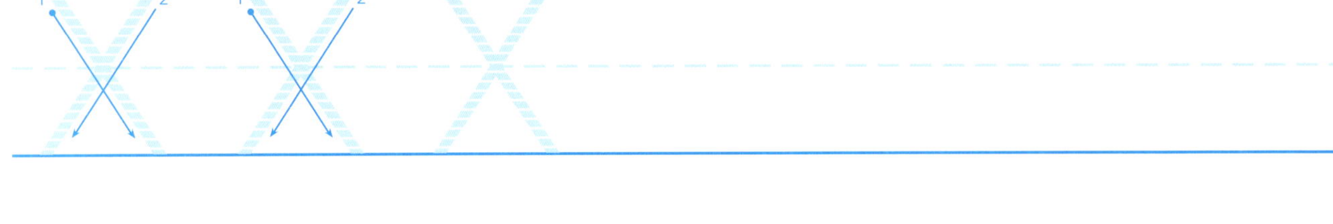

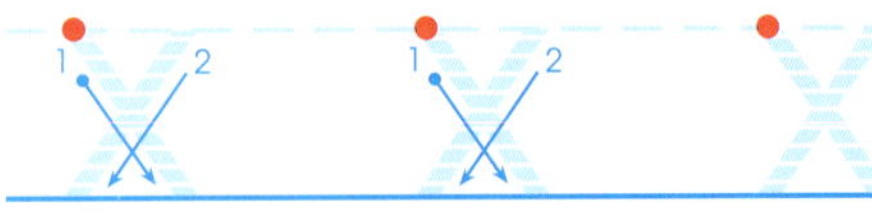

Color the picture.

Trace the letters to finish the sentence. Start at the red dots (●).

X is for x-ray fish.

CCSS.ELA-Literacy.RF.K.1.D

I can recognize all uppercase and lowercase letters in the alphabet.

Trace and write the letters.
Start at the red dot (●).

Y Y Y

y y y

Color the picture.

Trace the letters to finish the sentence. Start at the red dots (●).

Y is for yak.

I can recognize all uppercase and lowercase letters in the alphabet.

Trace and write the letters.
Start at the red dot (●).

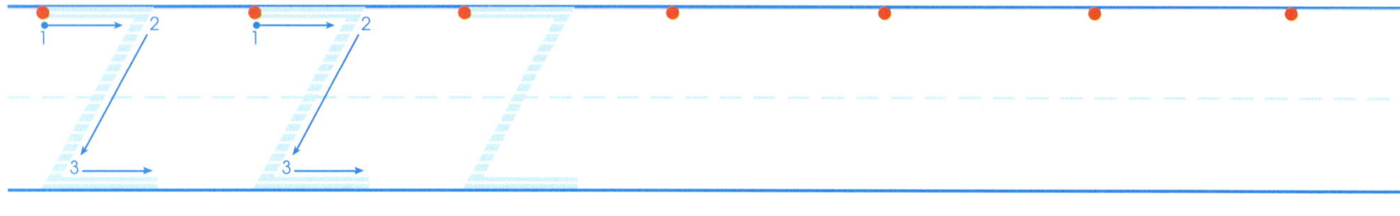

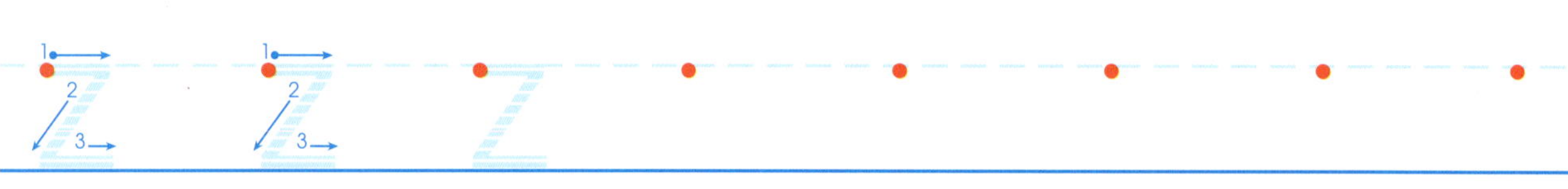

Color the picture.

Trace the letters to finish the sentence. Start at the red dots (●).

Z is for zebra.

Got it! OK Not yet

CCSS.ELA-Literacy.RF.K.1.D

I can recognize all uppercase and lowercase letters in the alphabet.

Say the name of each picture.
Underline the letters in each row that begin the name of the picture.

U J u a U

S z s S r

W v V v N

t H T f T

Got it! OK Not yet

I can recognize all uppercase and lowercase letters in the alphabet.

Draw a line from each uppercase letter to the matching lowercase letter.

U	w
V	v
W	x
X	u
Y	z
Z	y

Got it! OK Not yet

CCSS.ELA-Literacy.RF.K.1.D

I can recognize all uppercase and lowercase letters in the alphabet.

Connect the dots from **A** to **Z**.
Color the picture.

M N L O K P I J Q R H G S T E F U V D C X W A B Y Z

Got it! OK Not yet

I can recognize all uppercase and lowercase letters in the alphabet.

Which letters are missing?
Write in the missing uppercase letters.

A B C D E F G H I J K L M N O P Q R S T U V W X Y Z

A B ___ D ___

___ ___ H ___ ___ K

___ M ___ O ___

Q ___ ___ T ___ V

___ X ___ ___

Got it! OK Not yet

CCSS.ELA-Literacy.RF.K.1.D

I can understand that numbers and quantities are connected.

Trace and write the numbers.

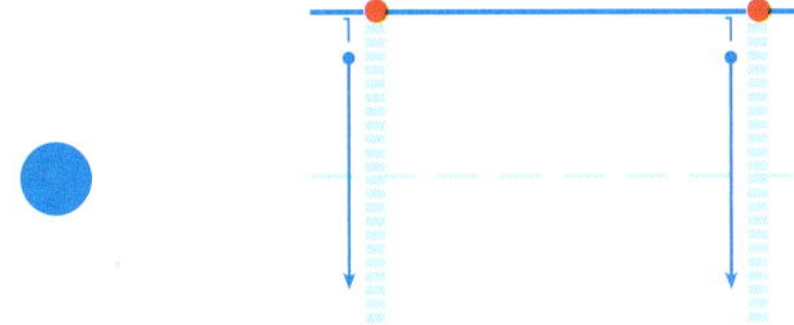

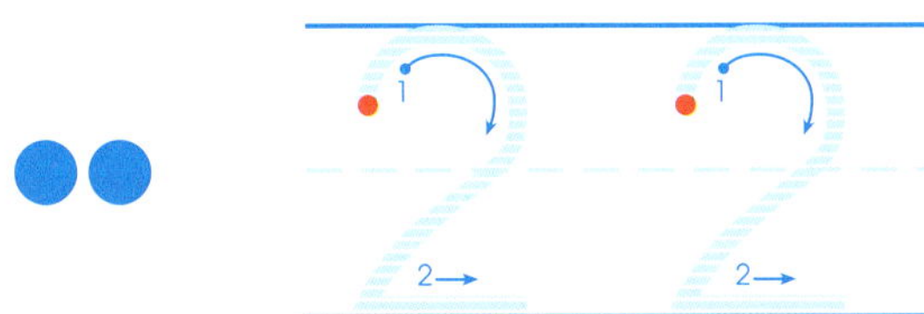

How many animals are there in each group? Write the numbers.

Got it! OK Not yet

You need:

I can understand that numbers and quantities are connected.

Find and place the stickers in the matching number boxes.

1

2

Got it!

OK

Not yet

CCSS.Math.Content.K.CC.B.4

I can understand that numbers and quantities are connected.

Trace and write the numbers.

How many birds are there in each group?
Write the numbers.

Got it!

OK

Not yet

I can understand that things in a group can be moved around and the total number will be the same.

It does not matter how the objects are arranged, they are still the same.

Got it! OK Not yet

CCSS.Math.Content.K.CC.B.4.B

I can understand that counting has to happen in a certain order.

You need:

Write the answers.

How many  are **inside** the room? ______________

How many  are **outside** the room? ______________

How many  are **over** the door? ______________

Got it!

OK

Not yet

I can understand that numbers and quantities are connected.

Zero means **there are none**.

 Trace and write the number.

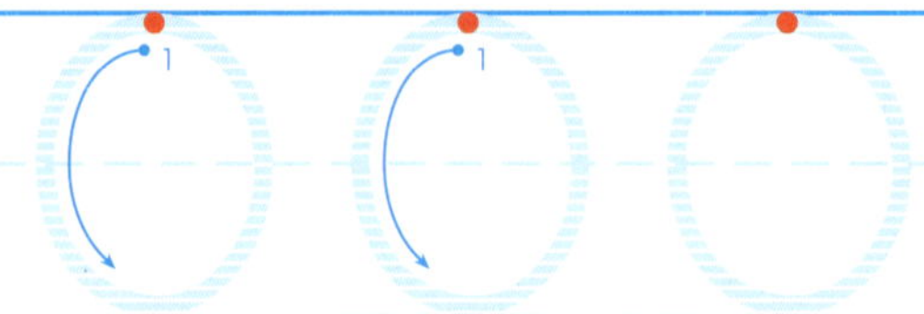

How many puppies are there in each group?
Write the number.

Got it! OK Not yet

CCSS.Math.Content.K.CC.B.4

I can understand that numbers and quantities are connected.

✓ Check the areas that have **0** kittens.

Got it! OK Not yet

I can understand that numbers and quantities are connected.

Trace and write the numbers.

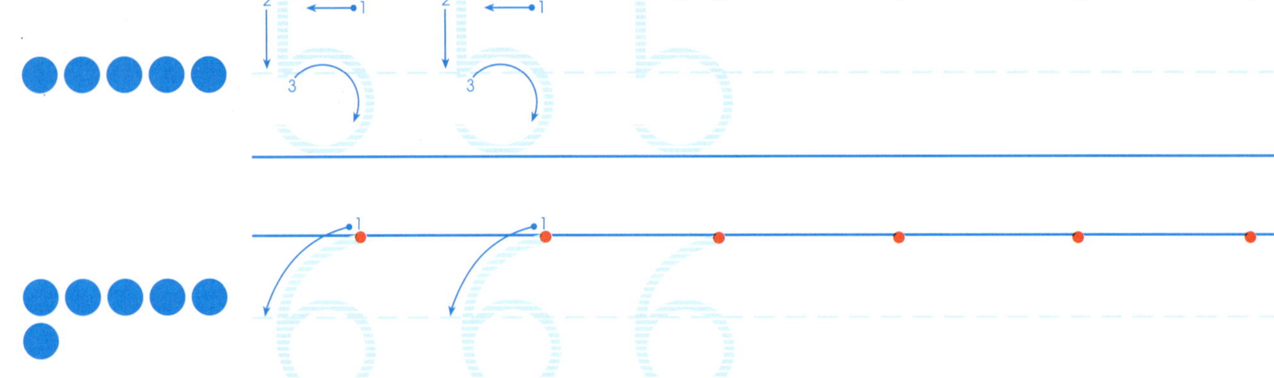

How many animals are there in each group?
Write the numbers.

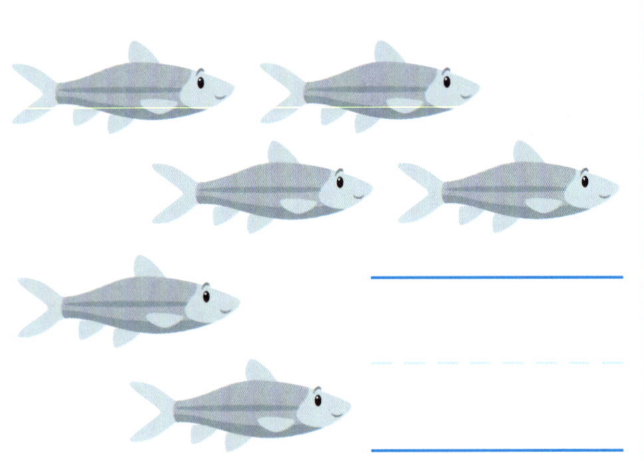

Got it! OK Not yet

CCSS.Math.Content.K.CC.B.4

I can understand that numbers and quantities are connected.

Count each group.
Circle the number.

4 5 6

4 5 6

4 5 6

4 5 6

4 5 6

Got it! OK Not yet

I can understand that the next number I say when I count means that there is one more.

Count the shapes.
Draw **1 more** shape.
Write how many shapes you have now.
The first one is done for you.

Count	Draw	Write

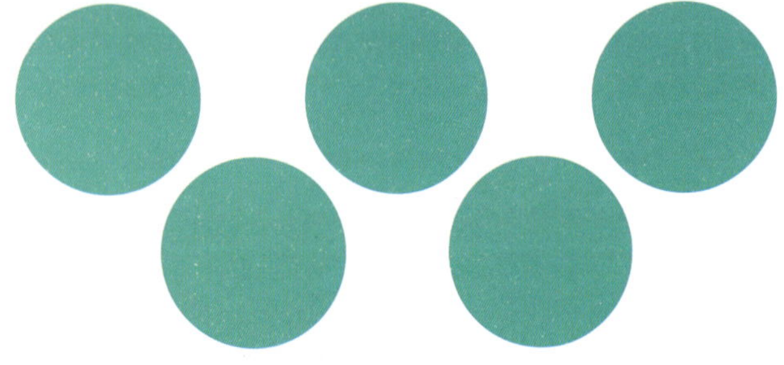	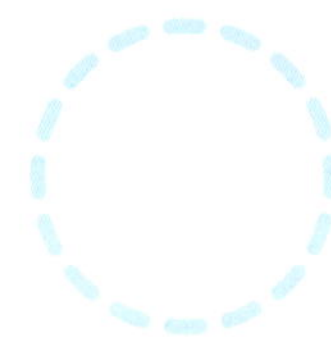	
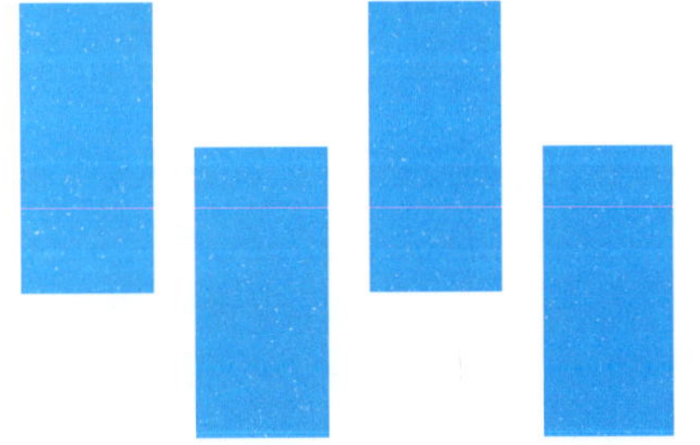		

Got it!

OK

Not yet

CCSS.Math.Content.K.CC.B.4.C

I can understand that numbers and quantities are connected.

Draw a line from each number to the correct group.
Write each number by the correct group.
The first one is done for you.

Online Extra:
To go to this activity, use your smartphone camera, hover over this code, and click on the link. Or go to: **anywhereteacher.com/qr/14162/06.**

Got it!

OK

Not yet

I can understand that numbers and quantities are connected.

Trace and write the numbers.

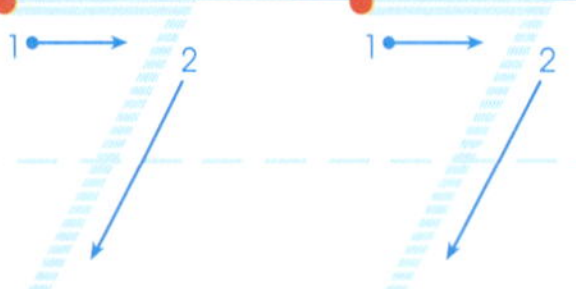

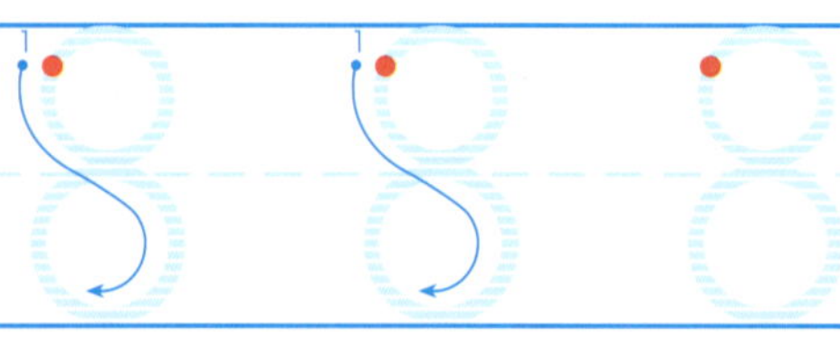

How many animals are there in each group? Write the numbers.

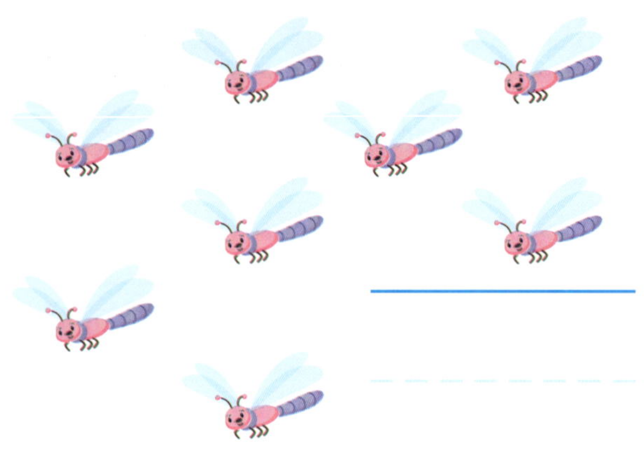

CCSS.Math.Content.K.CC.B.4

I can understand that numbers and quantities are connected.

Color 7 turtles green.

Color 8 ducks yellow.

Got it! OK Not yet

I can understand that the next number I say when I count means that there is one more.

Count each group.
Circle the group that has **1 more** than the first group in each row.

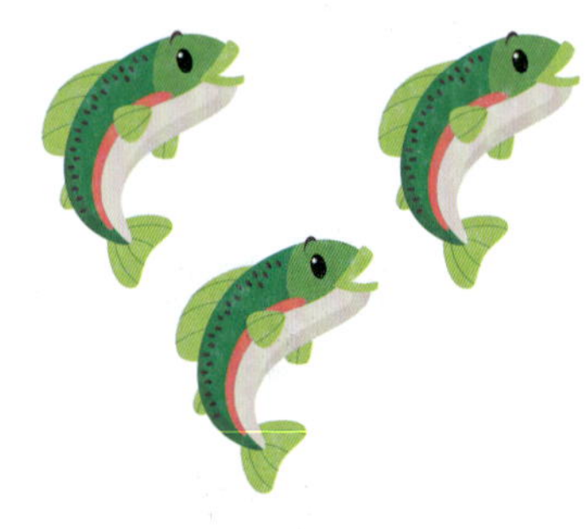

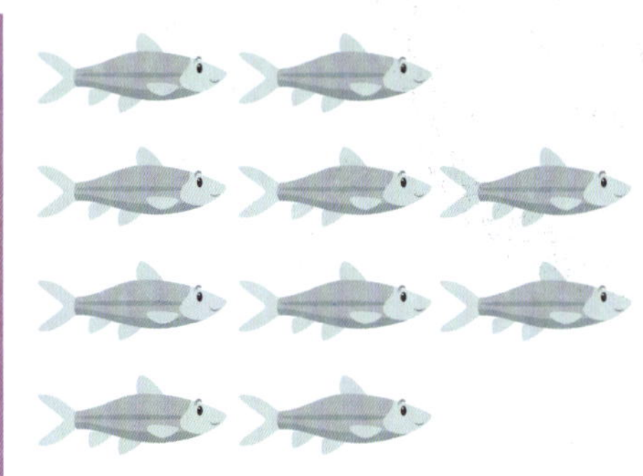

5

Got it!

OK

Not yet

CCSS.Math.Content.K.CC.B.4

I can understand that numbers and quantities are connected.

Trace and write the numbers.

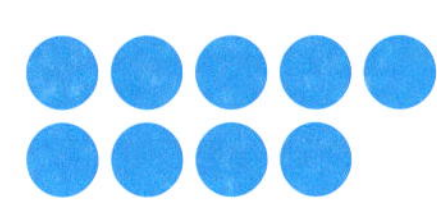

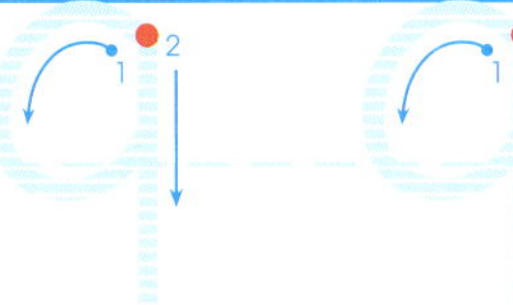

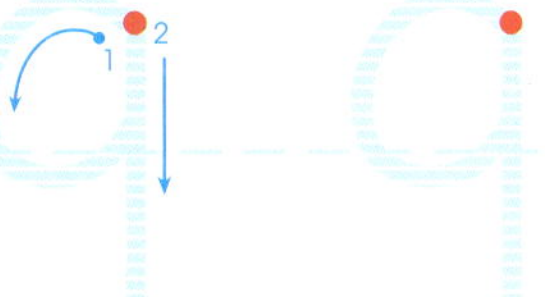

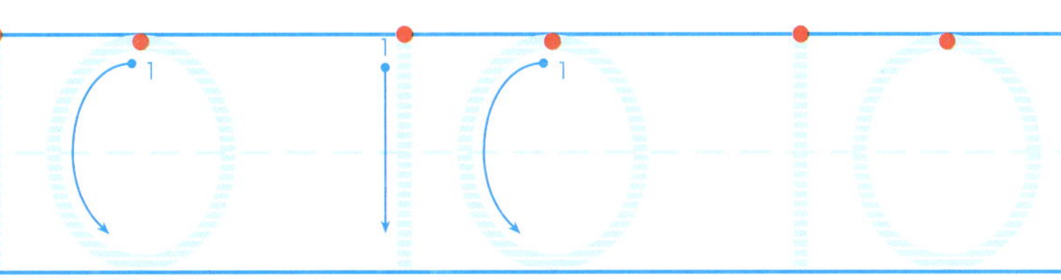

How many animals are there in each group?
Write the numbers.

Got it!

OK

Not yet

You need:

I can understand that numbers and quantities are connected.

Find and circle **9** [squirrel].

Find and place **10** [cardinal] stickers.

Got it! OK Not yet

CCSS.Math.Content.K.CC.B.4

I can understand that counting has to happen in a certain order.

Connect the dots from **1** to **10**.
Color the picture.

1 2 3 4 5 6 7 8 9 10

Got it! OK Not yet

I can understand that numbers and quantities are connected.

Count each group.
Color the boxes to match the number.
Write the number.

Count	Color	Write
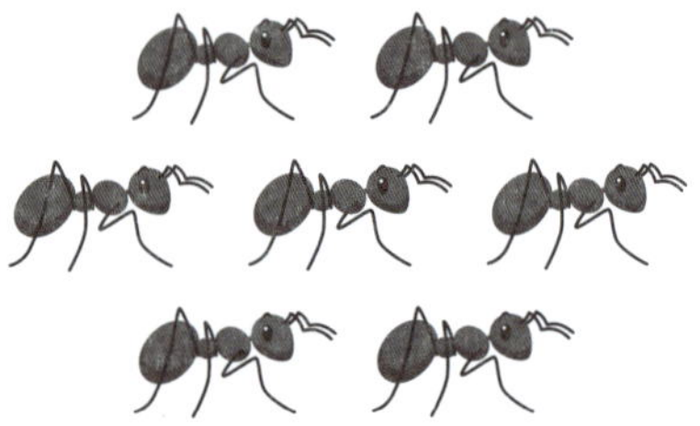		7

Got it! OK Not yet

CCSS.Math.Content.K.CC.B.4

I can understand that numbers and quantities are connected.

Write the answer.

How many [tree stump] can you find? ___

Got it! OK Not yet

You need:

I can point to the cover, title, and back cover on a book.

The **front cover** of the book has large words to tell the title. It has large pictures to show what the book is about.

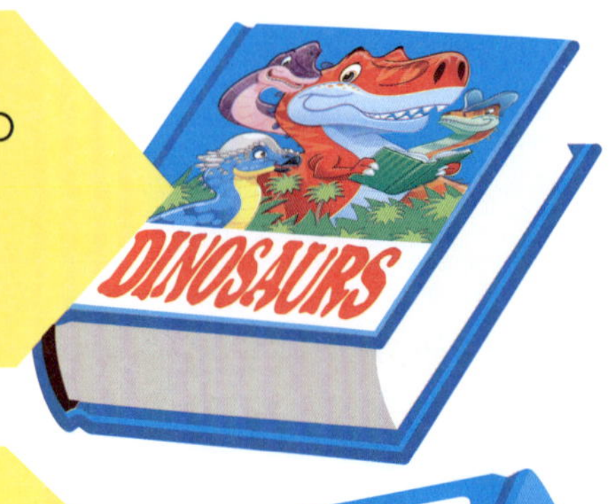

The **back cover** of a book usually has smaller words and smaller pictures.

The **spine** of a book usually has the title of the book on it.

✓ Check the front cover.

Circle the spine.

✗ Cross out the back cover.

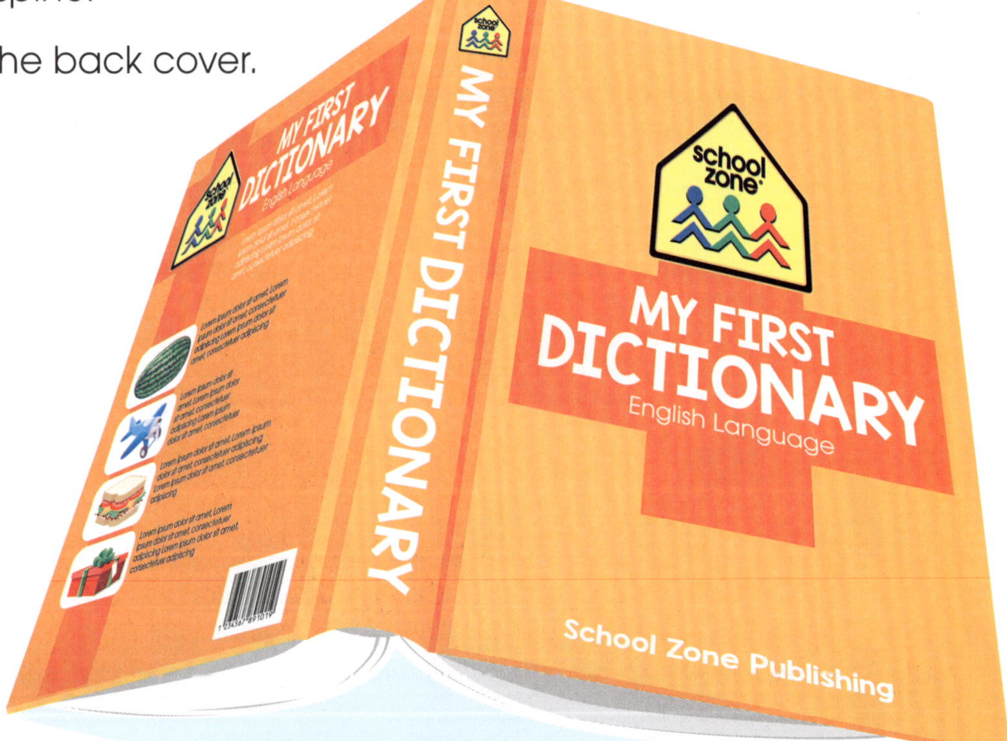

Got it!

OK

Not yet

CCSS.ELA-Literacy.RF.K.1

I can understand the job of an author and illustrator.

An **author** is the person who writes the words in a book.

An **illustrator** is the person who creates the pictures in a book.

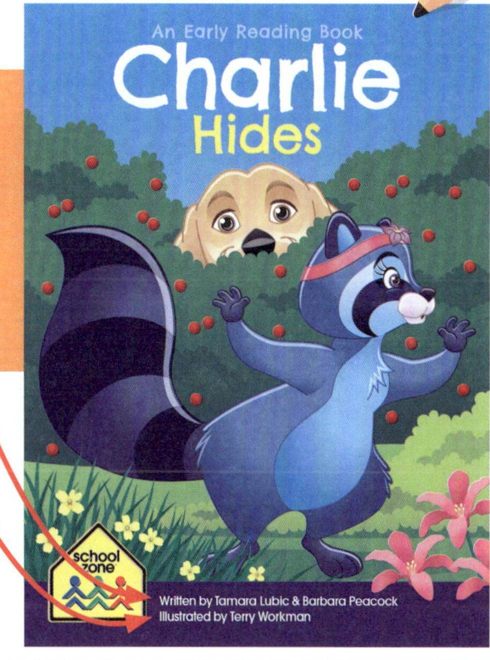

Online Extra:
To go to this activity, use your smartphone camera, hover over this code, and click on the link. Or go to: **anywhereteacher.com/qr/14162/01**.

Draw a line from **author** and **illustrator** to what each person did in the book.

Author

Illustrator

Got it!

OK

Not yet

I can point out different kinds of writing like storybooks and poems.

 Circle the books you would like to read.

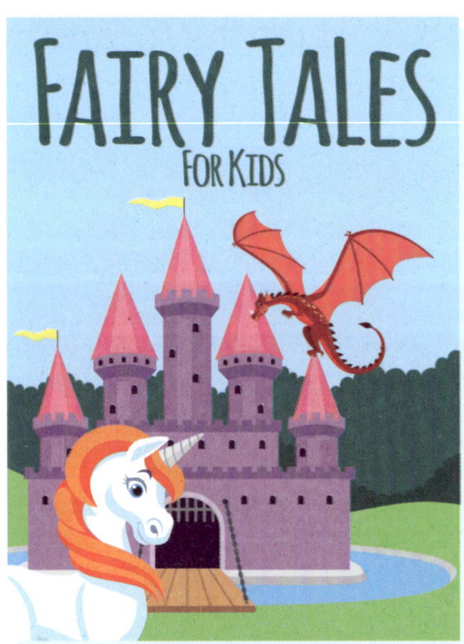

CCSS.ELA-Literacy.RL.K.5

I can read poetry.

Read the poems below.

 Circle the answers.

I have a new bike,
its color is red,
I rode it all day,
now it is time for
 or .

Look at me,
I swim all day,
I live in the sea,
my color is  or .

Extra Credit!
Go to the library and check out nursery rhymes, classic fairy tales, or poetry books.

 Got it!
 OK
 Not yet

I can be an active learner in fiction reading activities.

You need:

Read the book **Charlie Hides**.
Try to remember all of the important parts.

Parent Tip:
Use the press-out bookmark when reading with your child. Stop while reading and ask them some of the questions.

 Draw a picture of your favorite part of the story.

Got it! OK Not yet

CCSS.ELA-Literacy.RL.K.10

I can sort objects into different categories.

Cross out what **does not belong** in the tree.

Cross out what **does not belong** underwater.

Got it!

OK

Not yet

I can sort objects into different categories.

✗ Cross out what **does not belong** in each row.

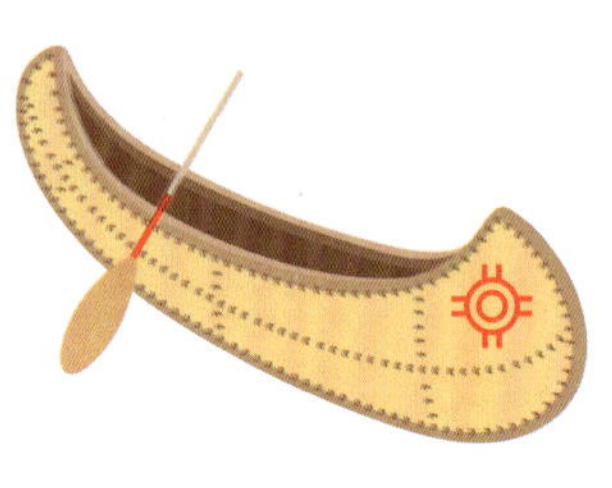  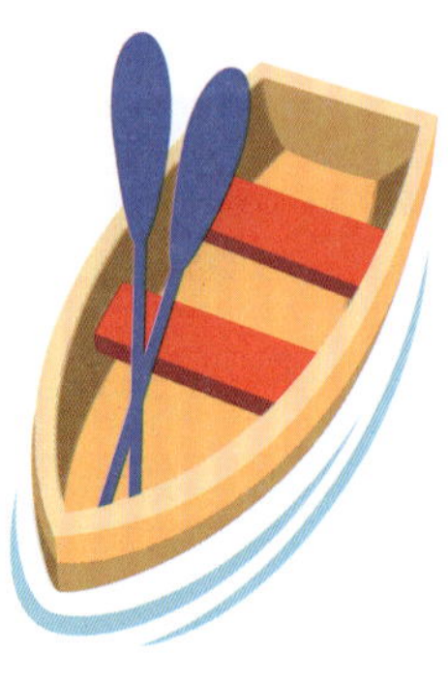 

Got it!

OK

Not yet

CCSS.Math.Content.K.MD.B.3

You need:

I can sort objects into different categories.

 Draw a line from each picture to where it **belongs**.

Animals

Plants

Got it!

OK

Not yet

You need:

I can sort objects into different categories.

Find and place each vehicle sticker to show where it does its job.

Got it! OK Not yet

CCSS.Math.Content.K.MD.B.3

You need:

I can correctly name shapes even when their sizes and positions are different.

Triangles are shapes that look like these:

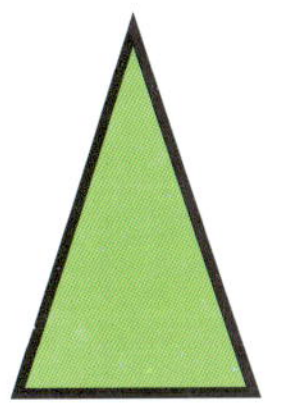

How many △ can you find? ______________

Got it! OK Not yet

I can correctly name shapes even when their sizes and positions are different.

You need:

A **square** is a shape that looks like this:

How many □ can you find? ____________

Got it! OK Not yet

CCSS.Math.Content.K.G.A.2

I can correctly name shapes even when their sizes and positions are different.

You need:

A **rectangle** is a shape that looks like this:

____

How many  ▭ can you find? ______________

Got it! OK Not yet

You need:

I can correctly name shapes even when their sizes and positions are different.

Color each △ blue.

Color each □ orange.

Color each ▭ green.

Got it! OK Not yet

CCSS.Math.Content.K.G.A.2

I can print many uppercase letters.

You need:

Circle the pictures that begin with the letter **A.**

Trace and write **A.**

Circle the pictures that begin with the letter **B.**

   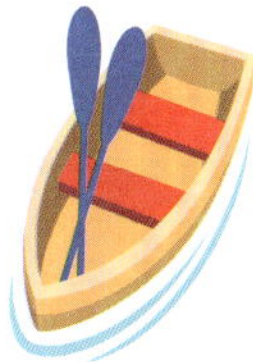

Trace and write **B.**

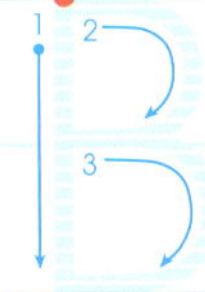

Got it! OK Not yet

CCSS.ELA-Literacy.L.K.1.A

I can print many uppercase letters.

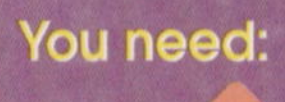

Circle the pictures that begin with the letter **C.**

Trace and write **C.**

D

DREAMING DINOSAUR

Circle the pictures that begin with the letter **D.**

Trace and write **D.**

Got it! OK Not yet

CCSS.ELA-Literacy.L.K.1.A

I can print many uppercase letters.

You need:

E
EXCELLENT EGGS

Circle the pictures that begin with the letter **E.**

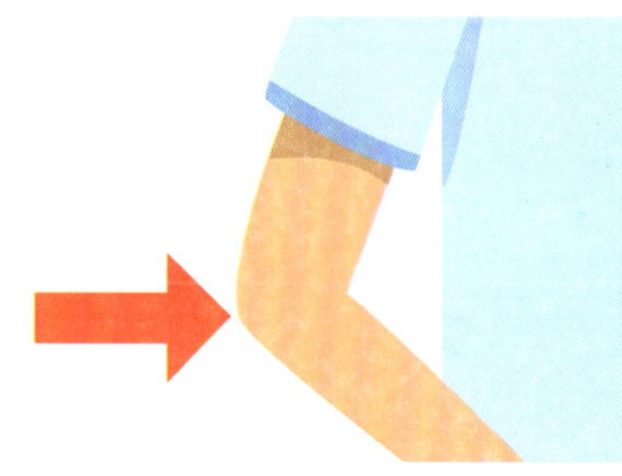

Trace and write **E.**

F
FURRY FRIENDS

Circle the pictures that begin with the letter **F.**

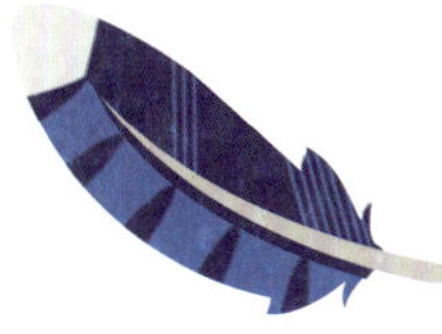

Trace and write **F.**

Got it! OK Not yet

I can print many uppercase letters.

You need:

Circle the pictures that begin with the letter **G.**

  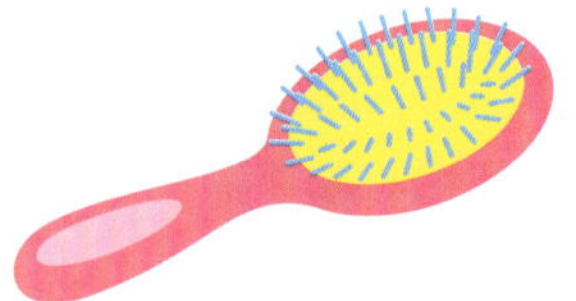 

Trace and write **G.**

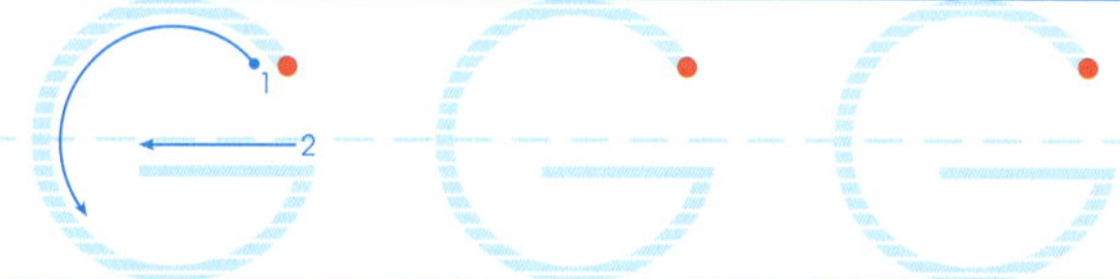

Circle the pictures that begin with the letter **H.**

Trace and write **H.**

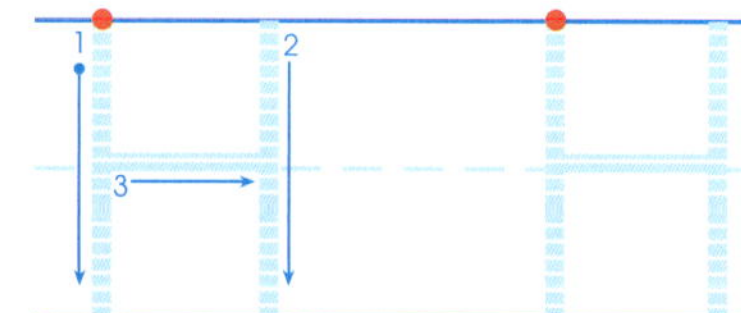

Got it! OK Not yet

CCSS.ELA-Literacy.L.K.1.A

I can print many uppercase letters.

You need:

Circle the pictures that begin with the letter **I.**

  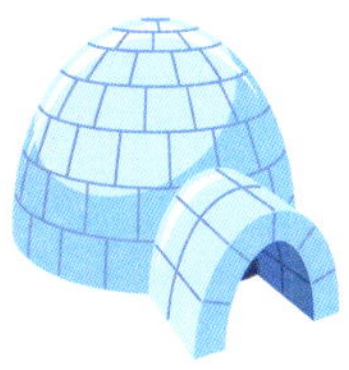 

Trace and write **I.**

Circle the pictures that begin with the letter **J.**

Trace and write **J.**

Got it! OK Not yet

You need:

I can print many uppercase letters.

Circle the pictures that begin with the letter **K.**

Trace and write **K.**

Circle the pictures that begin with the letter **L.**

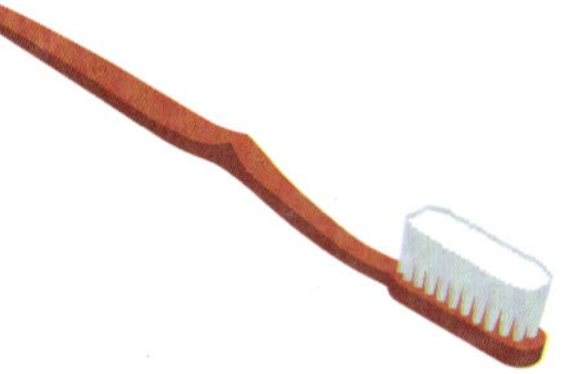

Trace and write **L.**

Got it! OK Not yet

CCSS.ELA-Literacy.L.K.1.A

I can print many uppercase letters.

You need:

Circle the pictures that begin with the letter **M.**

Trace and write **M.**

Circle the pictures that begin with the letter **N.**

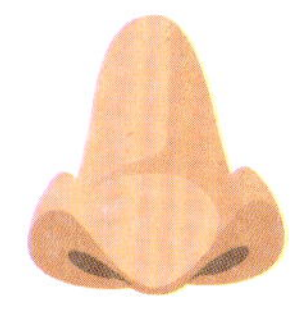

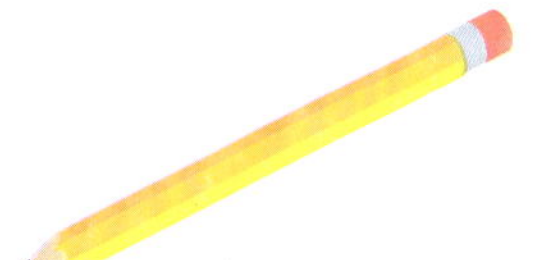

Trace and write **N.**

Got it!

OK

Not yet

You need:

I can print many uppercase letters.

Circle the pictures that begin with the letter **O.**

Trace and write **O.**

P

PEPPERONI PIZZA

Circle the pictures that begin with the letter **P.**

Trace and write **P.**

Got it!

OK

Not yet

CCSS.ELA-Literacy.L.K.1.A

I can print many uppercase letters.

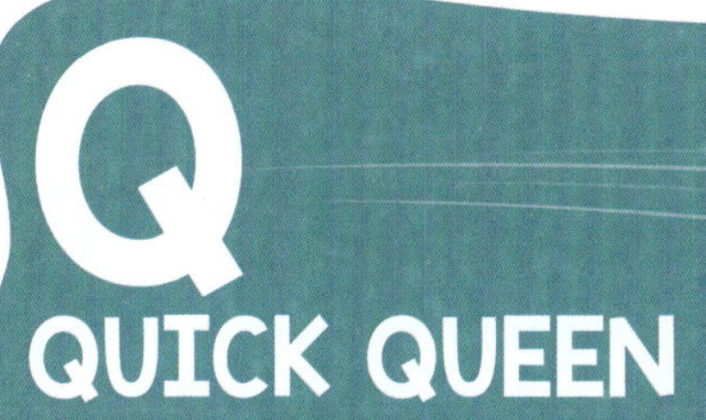

Circle the pictures that begin with the letter **Q.**

Trace and write **Q.**

Q Q Q

R

ROCKIN' ROBOT

Circle the pictures that begin with the letter **R.**

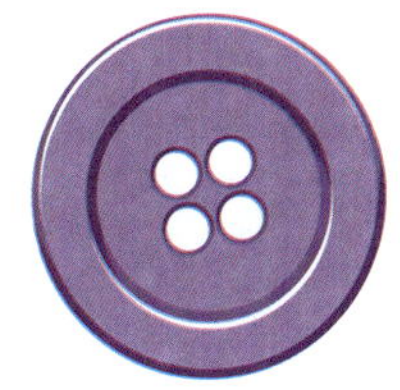

Trace and write **R.**

R R R

Got it!

OK

Not yet

You need:

I can print many uppercase letters.

S
SILLY SEAL

Circle the pictures that begin with the letter **S.**

Trace and write **S.**

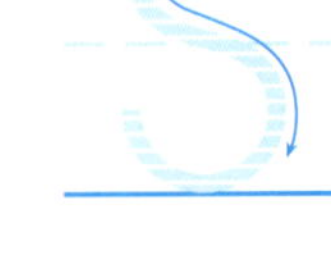

T
TEN TACOS

Circle the pictures that begin with the letter **T.**

Trace and write **T.**

Got it! OK Not yet

CCSS.ELA-Literacy.L.K.1.A

I can print many uppercase letters.

Circle the pictures that begin with the letter **U.**

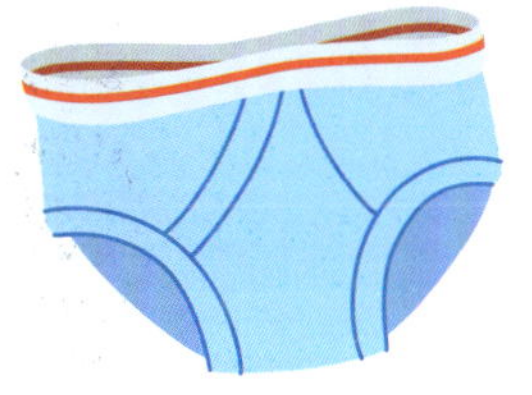

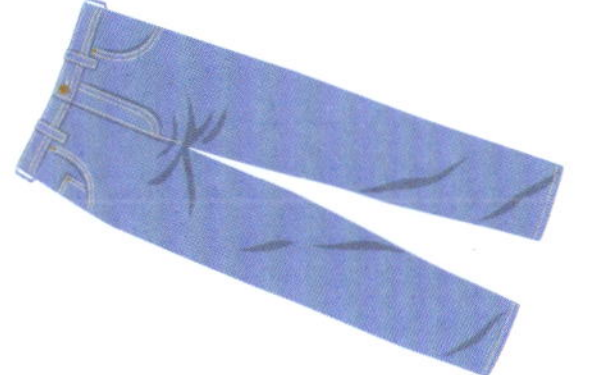

Trace and write **U.**

Circle the pictures that begin with the letter **V.**

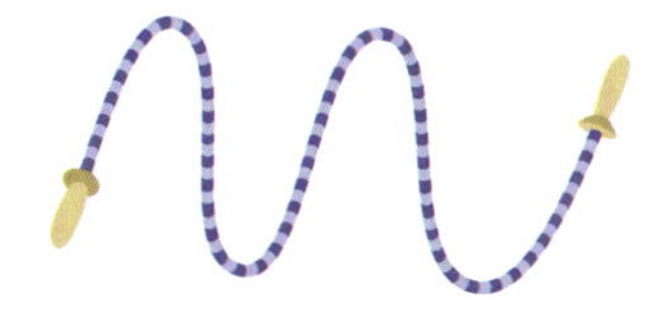

Trace and write **V.**

Got it! OK Not yet

You need:

I can print many uppercase letters.

Circle the pictures that begin with the letter **W.**

Trace and write **W.**

Circle the pictures that begin with the letter **X.**

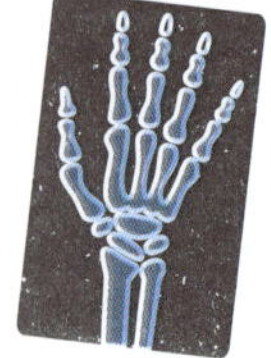   

Trace and write **X.**

Got it! OK Not yet

CCSS.ELA-Literacy.L.K.1.A

I can print many uppercase letters.

You need:

Circle the pictures that begin with the letter **Y.**

Trace and write **Y.**

Circle the pictures that begin with the letter **Z.**

Trace and write **Z.**

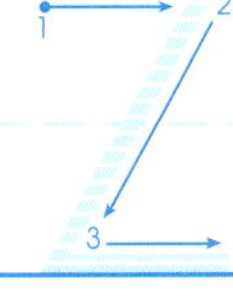

Got it! OK Not yet

I can print many uppercase letters.

You need:

C comes **after B.**
Write the letter that comes **after** each letter.
The first one is done for you.

A B C D E F G H I J K L M N O P Q R S T U V W X Y Z

B C

C

J

S

H

N

W

Y

Got it! OK Not yet

CCSS.ELA-Literacy.L.K.1.A

I can print many uppercase letters.

B comes **between A** and **C**.
Write the letter that comes **between** the letters.
The first one is done for you.

A B C D E F G H I J K L M N O P Q R S T U V W X Y Z

A B C   I __ K

P __ R   L __ N

T __ V   R __ T

X __ Z   D __ F

Got it! OK Not yet

I can print many uppercase letters.

You need:

A comes **before** B.
Write the letter that comes **before** each letter.
The first one is done for you.

A B C D E F G H I J K L M N O P Q R S T U V W X Y Z

A B

C

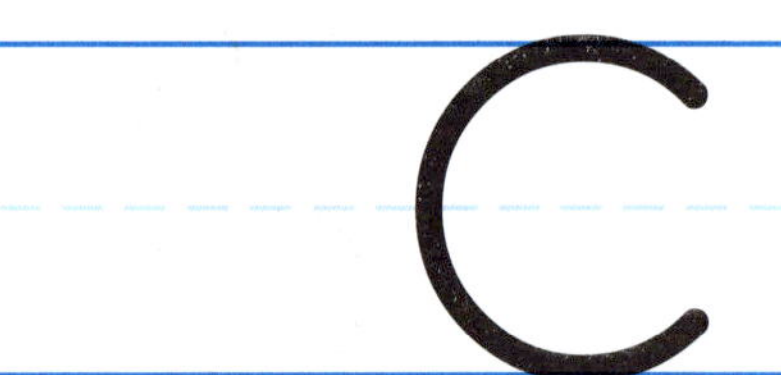

D

O

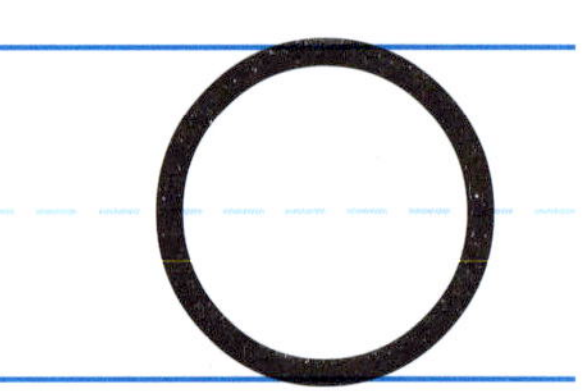

Y

R

G

M

Got it!

OK

Not yet

CCSS.ELA-Literacy.L.K.1.A

I can use smaller shapes to create one larger shape.

You can put two **triangles** together to make a new triangle.

Trace the **triangles** △.

Color the rest of the picture.

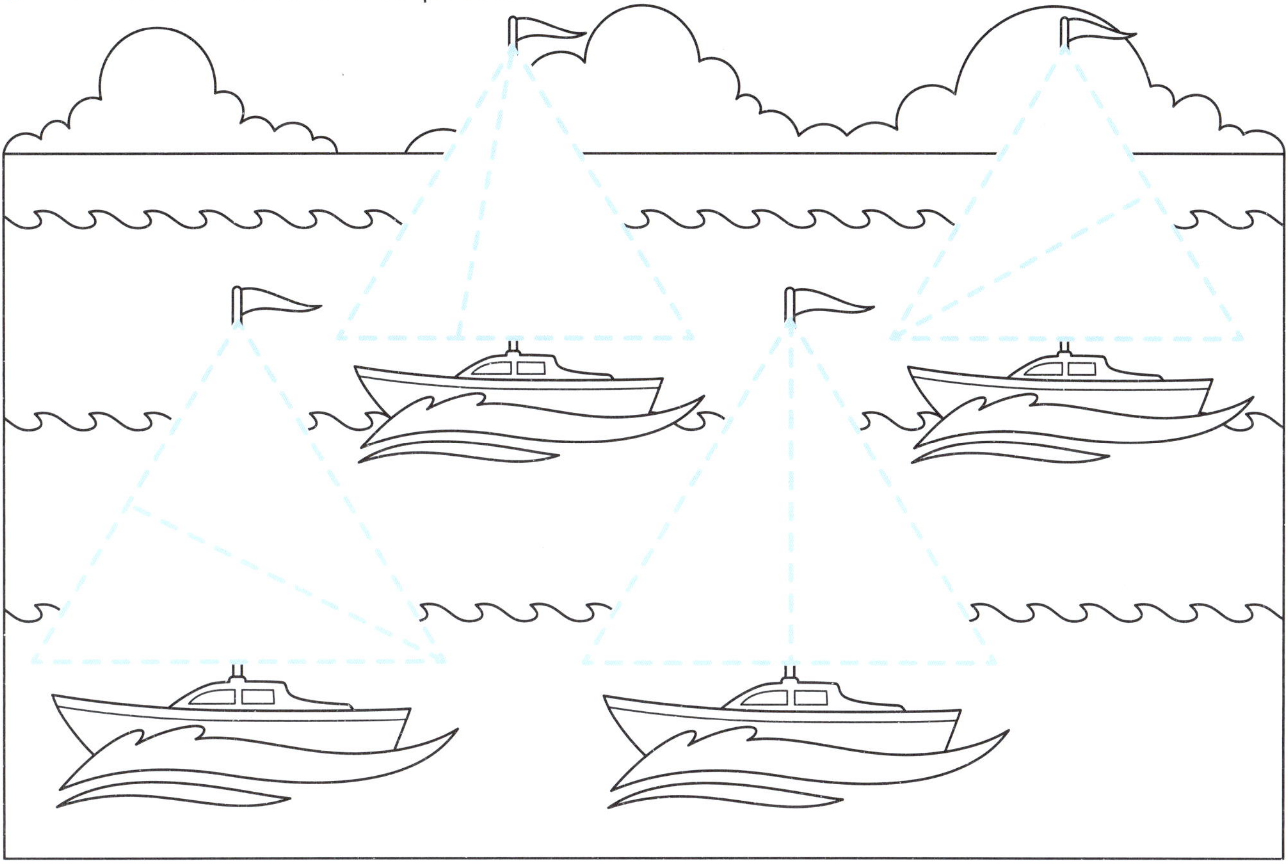

Finish drawing the △.

Draw a △.

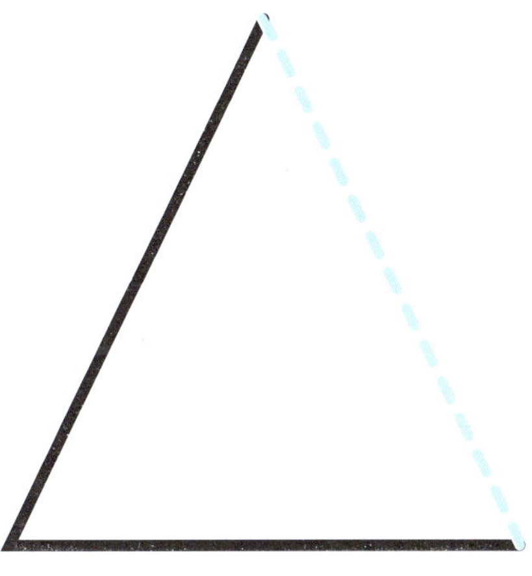

Got it! OK Not yet

I can use smaller shapes to create one larger shape.

You can put together two **squares** □□ to make a **rectangle** ▭.

Trace 2 **squares** □ on top of each other to make a **rectangle** birdhouse.

Color the rest of the picture.

Finish drawing the □.

Draw a □.

Got it! OK Not yet

CCSS.Math.Content.K.G.B.6

I can use smaller shapes to create one larger shape.

You can put two **rectangles** together to make a larger **rectangle**.

Trace the **rectangles** ▭.

Color the rest of the picture.

Finish drawing the ▭.

Draw a ▭.

Got it! OK Not yet

I can talk about a shape and what makes it unique.

You need:

Trace the **sides** of each shape.
Write how many **sides** each shape has.
The first one is done for you.

3 sides

square

____ sides

rectangle

____ sides

triangle

____ sides

Got it!

OK

Not yet

CCSS.Math.Content.K.G.B.4

You need:

I can talk about a shape and what makes it unique.

Sides are colored **blue**.
Corners are circled in **red**.

4 sides

4 corners

 Circle the shape with **3 sides** and **3 corners**.

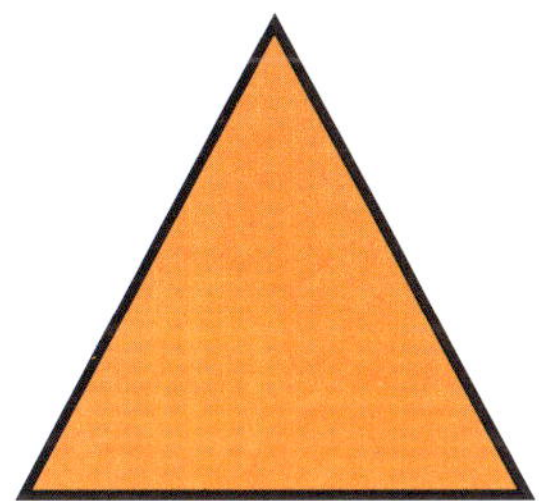

 Circle the shape with **4 sides** and **4 corners**.

 Circle the shape with **0 sides** and **0 corners**.

Got it!

OK

Not yet

CCSS.Math.Content.K.G.B.4

I can count syllables in spoken words.

You need:

cat **butter** **hamburger**

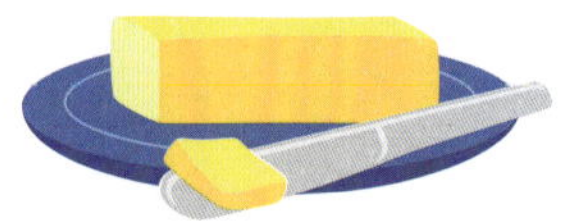

Clapping out the beats of the word allows you to count the syllables.

Online Extra: To go to this activity, use your smartphone camera, hover over this code, and click on the link. Or go to: **anywhereteacher.com/qr/14162/02**.

Say the name of each picture.

Clap and count the syllables.

Circle the number of syllables in each word.

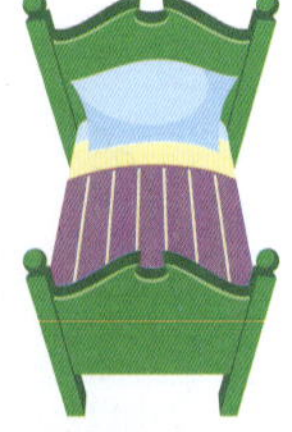

Got it! OK Not yet

CCSS.ELA-Literacy.RF.K.2.B

I can count syllables in spoken words.

You need:

Say the name of each picture.

Clap and count the syllables.

Circle the number of syllables in each word.

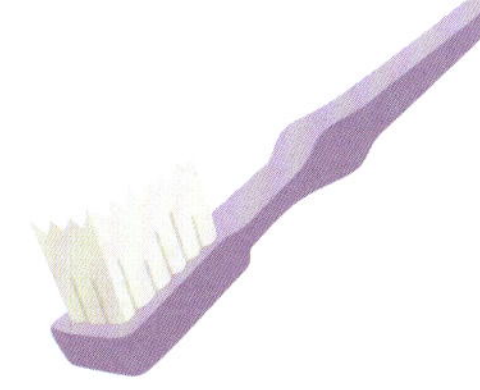

 Got it!

 OK

 Not yet

I can count syllables in spoken words.

Say the name of each picture.

Clap and count the syllables.

Circle the number of syllables in each word.

I can write and add to complete sentences with an adult and/or other kindergarteners.

A **personal narrative** is a story about something that happened to you and also includes a *feeling*.

Billy wrote a story about a time when he was happy.

One day I went to the pet store.

I looked at all the pets.

I picked a cat.
I felt ________.

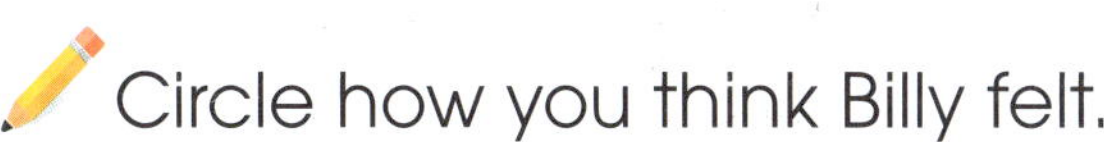 Circle how you think Billy felt.

happy

sad

Got it!

OK

Not yet

CCSS.ELA-Literacy.L.K.1.F

I can write and add to complete sentences with an adult and/or other kindergarteners.

Mary wrote a story.
Help her add a *feeling* to her story.

Today I got ice cream.

My ice-cream fell on the ground.

I picked it up.
I felt ________.

Circle how you think Mary felt.

sad

angry

frustrated

Got it!

OK

Not yet

CCSS.ELA-Literacy.L.K.1.F

You need: 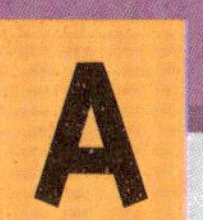

I can recognize and produce rhyming words.

A Read each word.
Place alphabet press-out pieces in the boxes to make words that rhyme with the first word.

example: 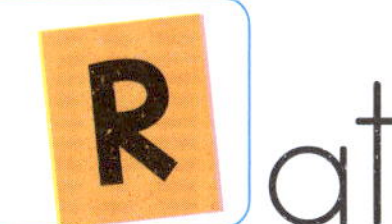 at

cat rhymes with  at

ball rhymes with  all

well rhymes with 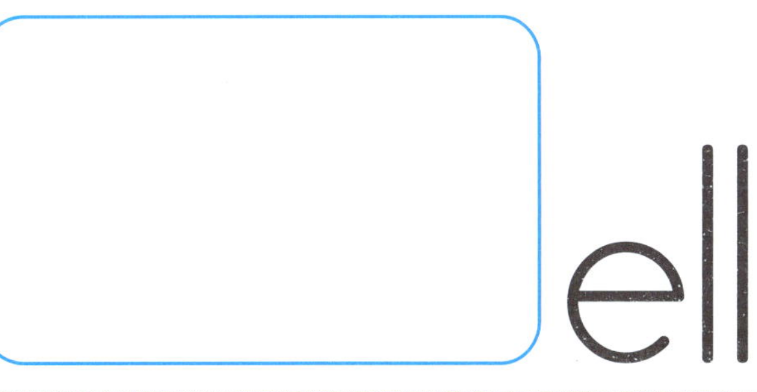 ell

frog rhymes with  og

 Got it!
 OK
 Not yet

You need:

I can recognize and produce rhyming words.

Say the name of each picture.
Color the **2** pictures that **rhyme** in each group.

CCSS.ELA-Literacy.RF.K.2.B

Two of a Kind

You need:

Look at each of the pictures.

Circle the two pictures that are the same.

Got it! OK Not yet

I can write, draw, and tell a story from my life that includes events in order and my reaction to what happened.

Read each story and answer the questions.

One day I went to the fun park.
I wanted to ride the roller coaster.
I felt ___________.

 Circle how you think you would feel.

excited

worried

afraid

It was my birthday.
I opened a gift.
I felt ___________.

 Circle how you think you would feel.

happy

surprised

silly

Got it!

OK

Not yet

CCSS.ELA-Literacy.W.K.1

I can write, draw, and tell a story from my life that includes events in order and my reaction to what happened.

Pictures in a personal narrative help to tell the story.

Carlos wrote a story about a time he was excited. Help him add details to his pictures.

I was making a sandcastle on the beach.

A big wave came and left a surprise.

Draw a picture on the sandcastle of what the surprise was.

I put it on my sandcastle. I was excited!

Got it!

OK

Not yet

I can write, draw, and tell a story from my life that includes events in order and my reaction to what happened.

Read the story and answer the questions.

I went for a walk down my street.

I heard a loud noise.

Draw a picture of what would make a loud noise.

I saw a ______________________.

I felt ____________.

Circle how you think you would feel?

happy

excited

afraid

I can capitalize the first word in a sentence and the pronoun I.

Write an uppercase letter to start each sentence and the pronoun **I**.

O ne day I went to the bookstore with my mom.

W e looked at all of the books.

W e picked a book.

I felt happy.

Got it! OK Not yet

I can show that I understand punctuation, capital letters, and spelling when writing.

A **telling sentence** begins with a capital letter and ends with a period (.).

Write an uppercase letter to start each sentence.
Write a period (.) at the end of each sentence.
The first one is done for you.

Our dog is hungry.

__ad brings food__

__kip eats quickly__

__ood goes on the floor__

__ogs are messy__

__ow I need to clean up__

CCSS.ELA-Literacy.L.K.2

I can show that I understand punctuation, capital letters, and spelling when writing.

An **asking sentence** begins with a capital letter and ends with a question mark (**?**).

Write an uppercase letter to start each sentence.
Write a question mark (**?**) at the end of each sentence.
The first one is done for you.

Is Mom home?

W here did she go ___

D id she bake cookies ___

C an I have one ___

H ow many did you eat ___

A re they still warm ___

I can show that I understand punctuation, capital letters, and spelling when writing.

Write your own **personal narrative**. Be sure to include a feeling and words that help to tell the story. Use capital letters and punctuation.

Draw pictures to help tell your story.

1

2

Then,

Continue on next page

CCSS.ELA-Literacy.L.K.2

Parent Tip:
Make your child feel like an author and help them share their writing with relatives through technology.

3

Last,

Writing Checklist:

- [ ] I told my story in order.
- [ ] I used a capital letter at the beginning of each sentence.
- [ ] I added pictures.
- [ ] I used a (.) or (!) at the end of each sentence.

Got it!

OK

Not yet

Let's have some fun!

Help Oba swim to the crab.
Draw a line through the maze from **start** to **finish**.

Start

Finish

Got it! OK Not yet

I can capitalize the first word in a sentence and the pronoun I.

Cut out the booklet pages below and fold along the center line. Combine these pages with the booklet pages from page 127 to make a book.

Write the pronoun **I** in the blanks to complete the sentences. Then read the book out loud.

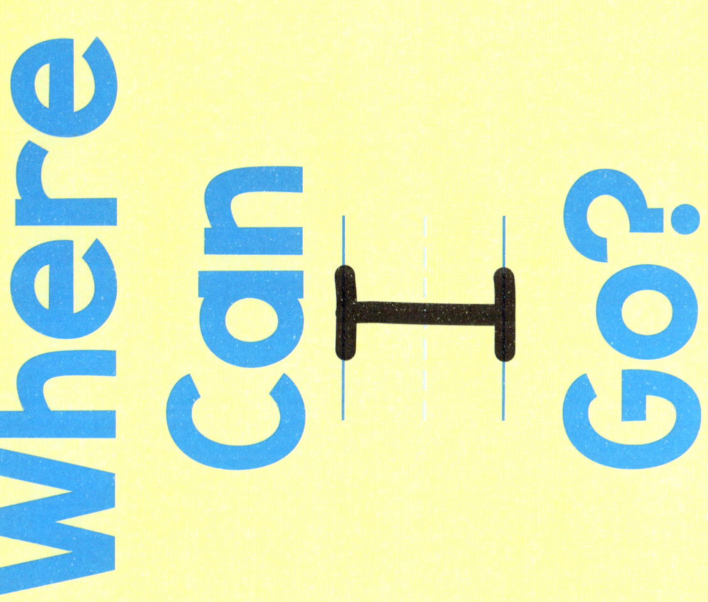

Fold along this line.

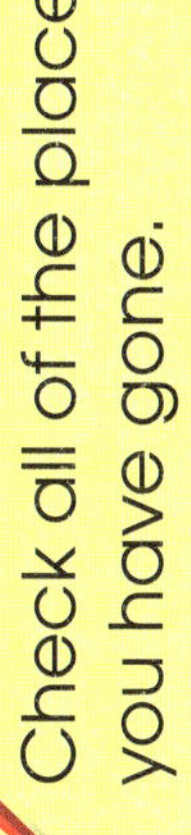

Park

Library

Beach

Store

Zoo

Home

Can ____ go to the park?

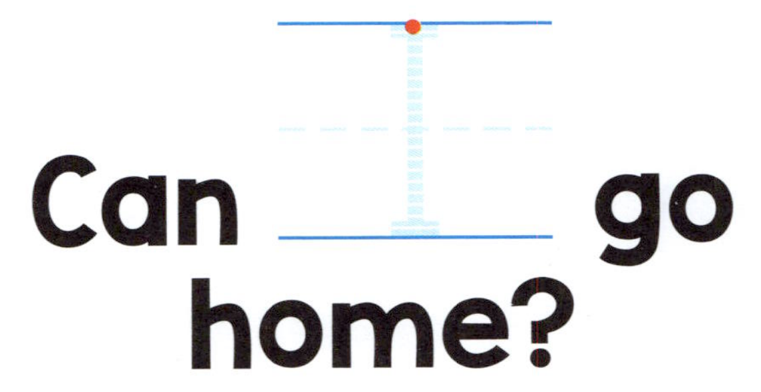

Can ____ go home?

CCSS.ELA-Literacy.L.K.2.A

I can capitalize the first word in a sentence and the pronoun I.

Cut out the booklet pages below and fold along the center line. Combine these pages with the booklet pages from page 125 to make a book.

Write the pronoun **I** in the blanks to complete the sentences. Then read the book out loud.

Can ______ go to the beach?

Fold along this line.

Can ______ go to the library?

Can ______ go
to the store?

Can ______ go
to the zoo?

I can develop self-control.

(sharing, taking turns, following rules, empathy, respecting others' space and property)

 Circle the emotion that matches the picture.

Happy Sad Mad

Happy Sad Mad

Happy Sad Mad

Happy Sad Mad

Online Extra:

To go to this activity, use your smartphone camera, hover over this code, and click on the link. Or go to: **anywhereteacher.com/qr/14162/03.**

Got it! OK Not yet

I can develop self-control.
(sharing, taking turns, following rules, empathy, respecting others' space and property)

 Circle the emotion that matches the picture.

Excited Disgusted Surprised

Excited Disgusted Surprised

Excited Disgusted Surprised

Excited Disgusted Surprised

Got it!

OK

Not yet

I can tell the characters, settings, and important events in a story with help.

You need:

Read the book **Charlie Hides**.

Circle all of the characters in the book **Charlie Hides**.

Circle the setting where the story took place.

Check what happened first in the book.

Got it!

OK

Not yet

I can read and understand kindergarten books.

You need:

Parents:
Please read the book **Charlie Hides** to your child.
Then ask the following questions.

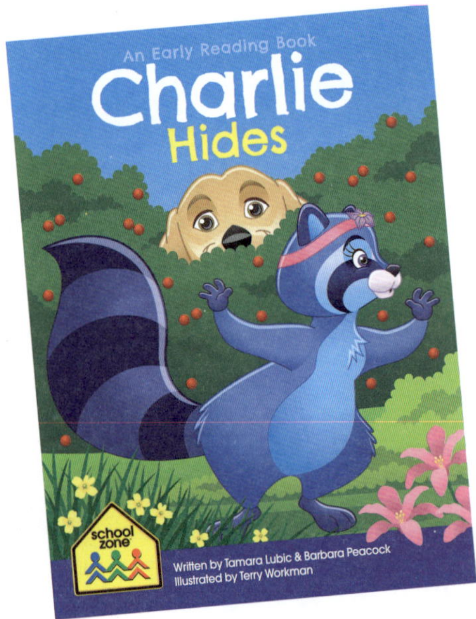

Why did the author write this book?

To tell a funny story about a dog playing hide and seek.

To teach you about a barn.

Who is hiding?

Violet

Charlie

What rhymes with log?

dog

barn

Where did Violet find Charlie?

cornfield

in the barn

Did you like reading the book **Charlie Hides**?

yes **no**

Got it!

OK

Not yet

CCSS.ELA-Literacy.RF.K.4

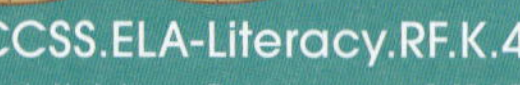

I can understand that numbers and quantities are connected.

Trace and write the numbers.

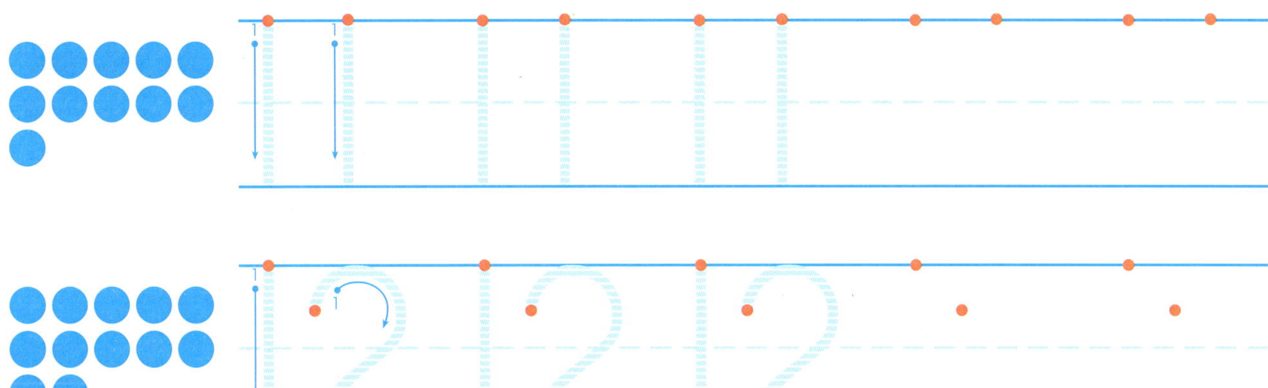

How many fish are there in each group?
Write the numbers.

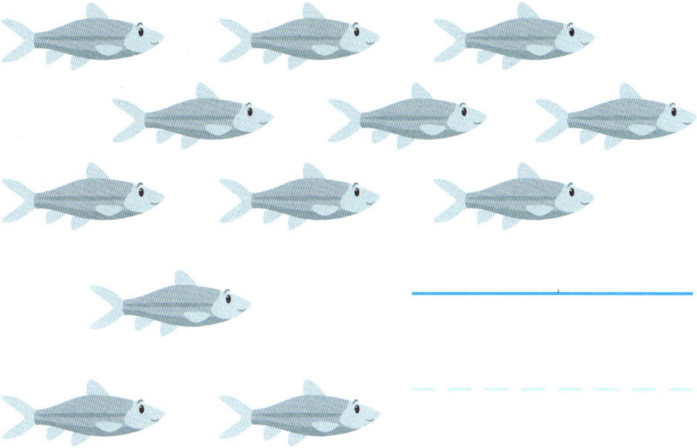

Got it! OK Not yet

I can understand that numbers and quantities are connected.

Find and circle the hidden pictures.

baseball bowling ball volleyball soccer ball basketball

CCSS.Math.Content.K.CC.B.4

You need:
Write the answer.
How many can you find?
Got it!
OK
Not yet

I can understand that numbers and quantities are connected.

You need:

 Trace and write the numbers.

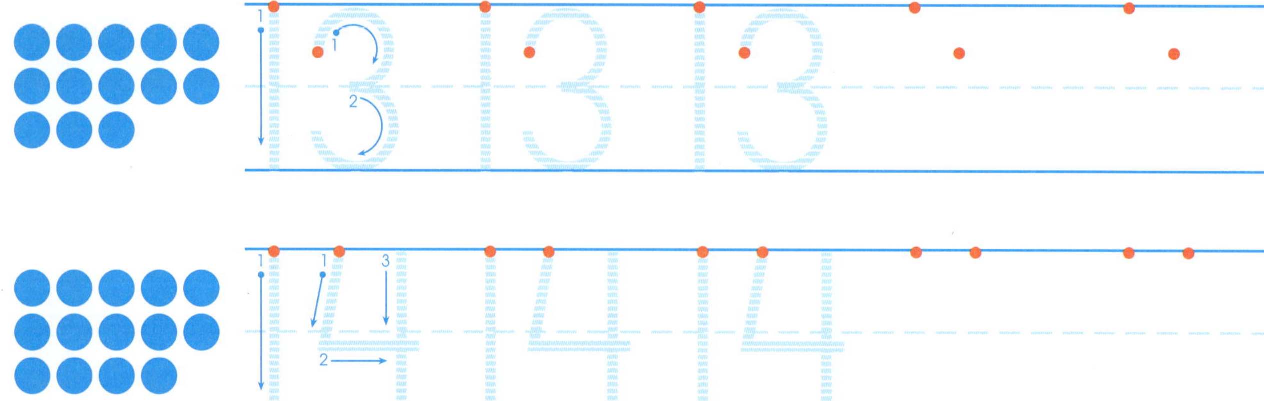

How many balloons are there in each group?
Write the numbers.

CCSS.Math.Content.K.CC.B.4

I can understand that numbers and quantities are connected.

Color the balloons with **13** on them green.

Color the balloons with **14** on them orange.

14 13 14 14 13 14 13 14 13 13 14 13

Got it! OK Not yet

I can understand that numbers and quantities are connected.

Trace and write the numbers.

How many marbles are there in each group?
Write the numbers.

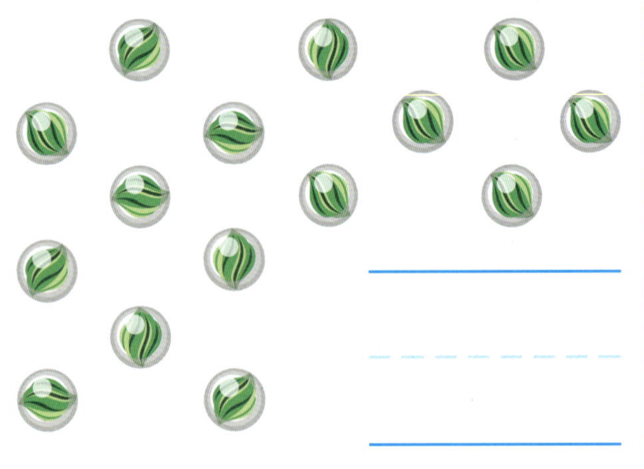

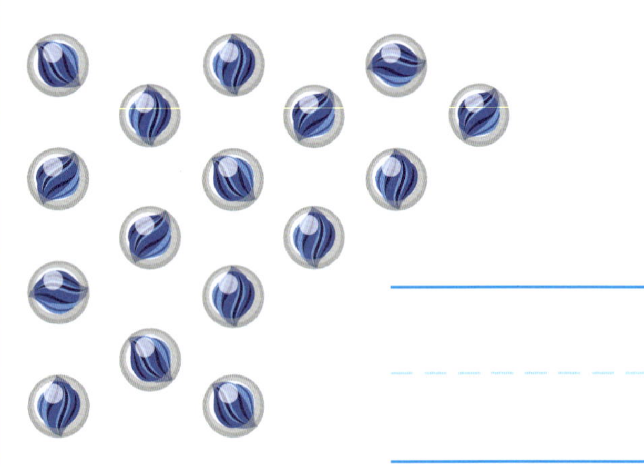

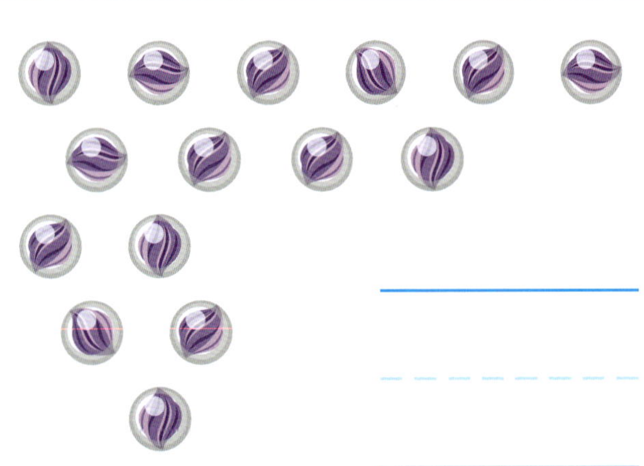

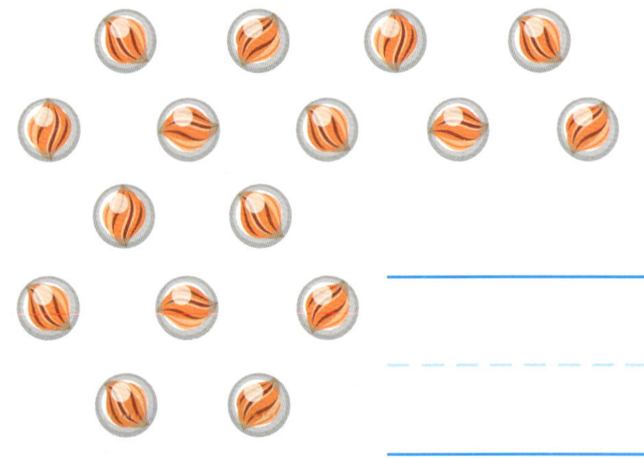

Got it! OK Not yet

CCSS.Math.Content.K.CC.B.4

I can understand that numbers and quantities are connected.

 Draw a line from each group to the matching number.

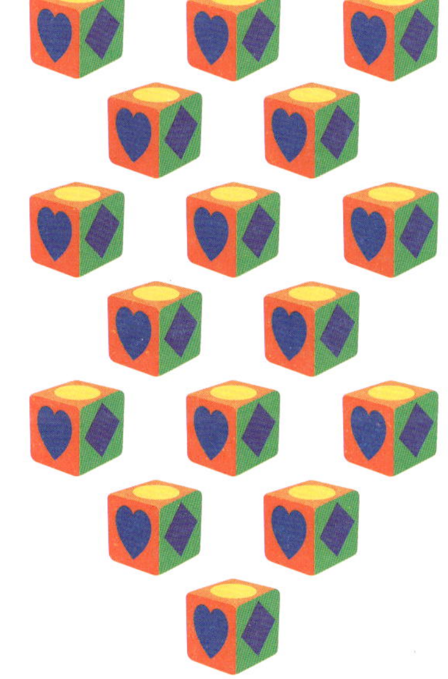

Got it!

OK

Not yet

CCSS.Math.Content.K.CC.B.4

I can understand that numbers and quantities are connected.

 Trace and write the numbers.

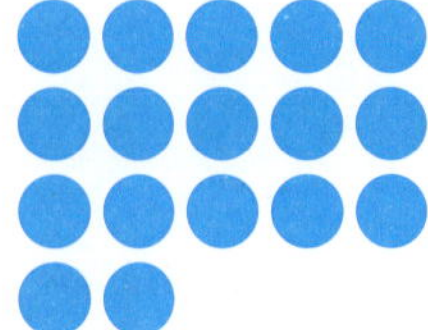

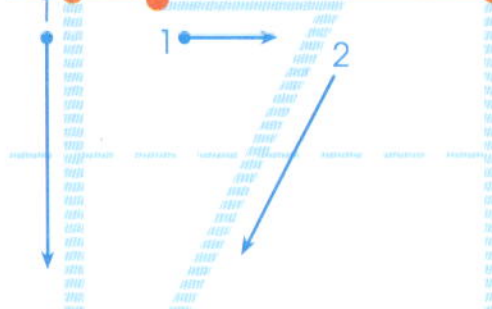

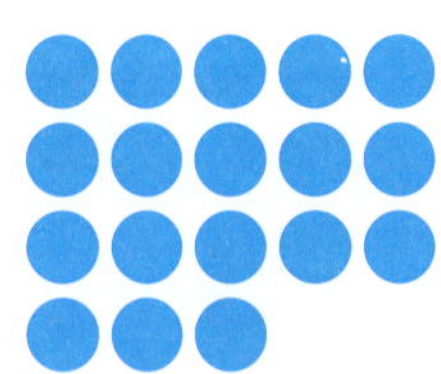

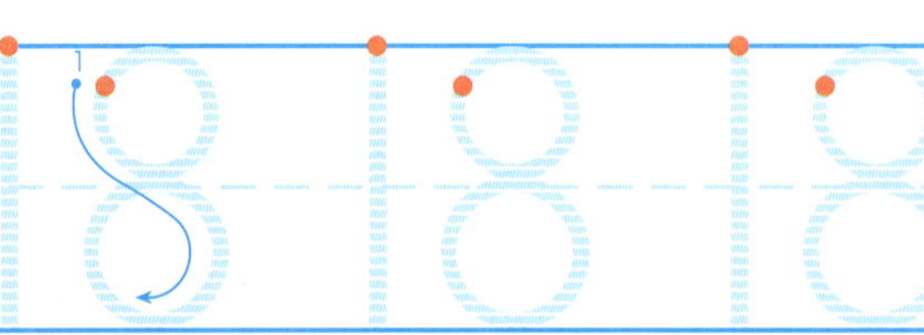

How many animals are there in each group?
Write the numbers.

CCSS.Math.Content.K.CC.B.4

BOOK 2

You need:

I can understand that numbers and quantities are connected.

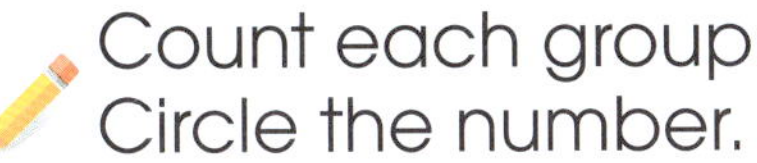

Count each group.
Circle the number.

Got it! OK Not yet

You need:

I can understand that numbers and quantities are connected.

 Trace and write the numbers.

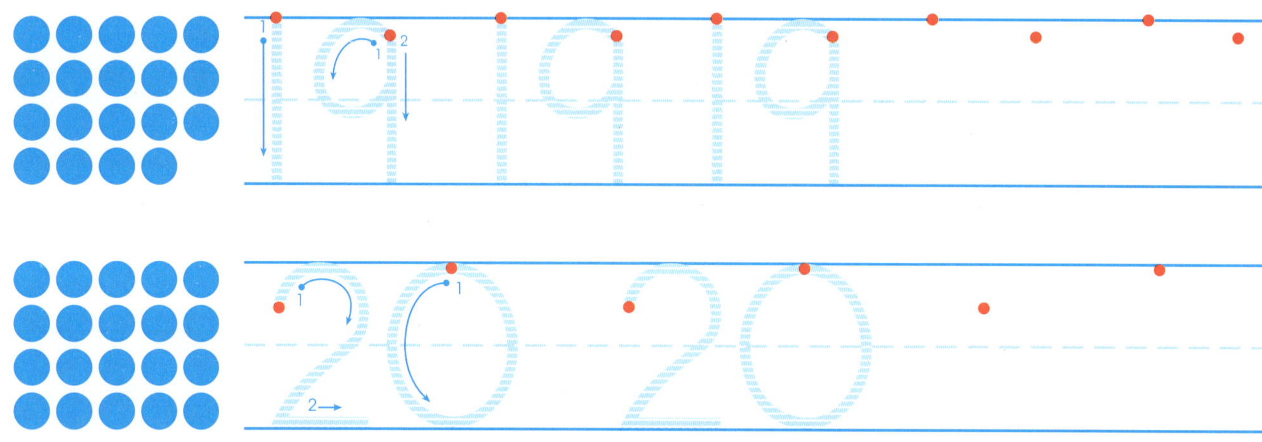

How many things are there in each group?
Write the numbers.

Got it!

OK

Not yet

CCSS.Math.Content.K.CC.B.4

I can understand that numbers and quantities are connected.

Color the leaves with **19** on them yellow.

Color the leaves with **20** on them red.

You need:

I can understand that counting has to happen in a certain order.

The number **14** comes **after** the number **13**.

Write the number that comes after.

17 18

Got it!

OK

Not yet

CCSS.Math.Content.K.CC.B.4

I can count to 20 by ones and tens.

You need:

Count to **20**.
Write the missing numbers.
Circle the numbers **10** and **20**.

1			4		6	7		9	
	12	13		15			18		20

Color the picture.

20

Got it! OK Not yet

I can blend together syllables in spoken words.

Say the name of each picture.
Find and place the BA syllable stickers under each picture in the correct order.

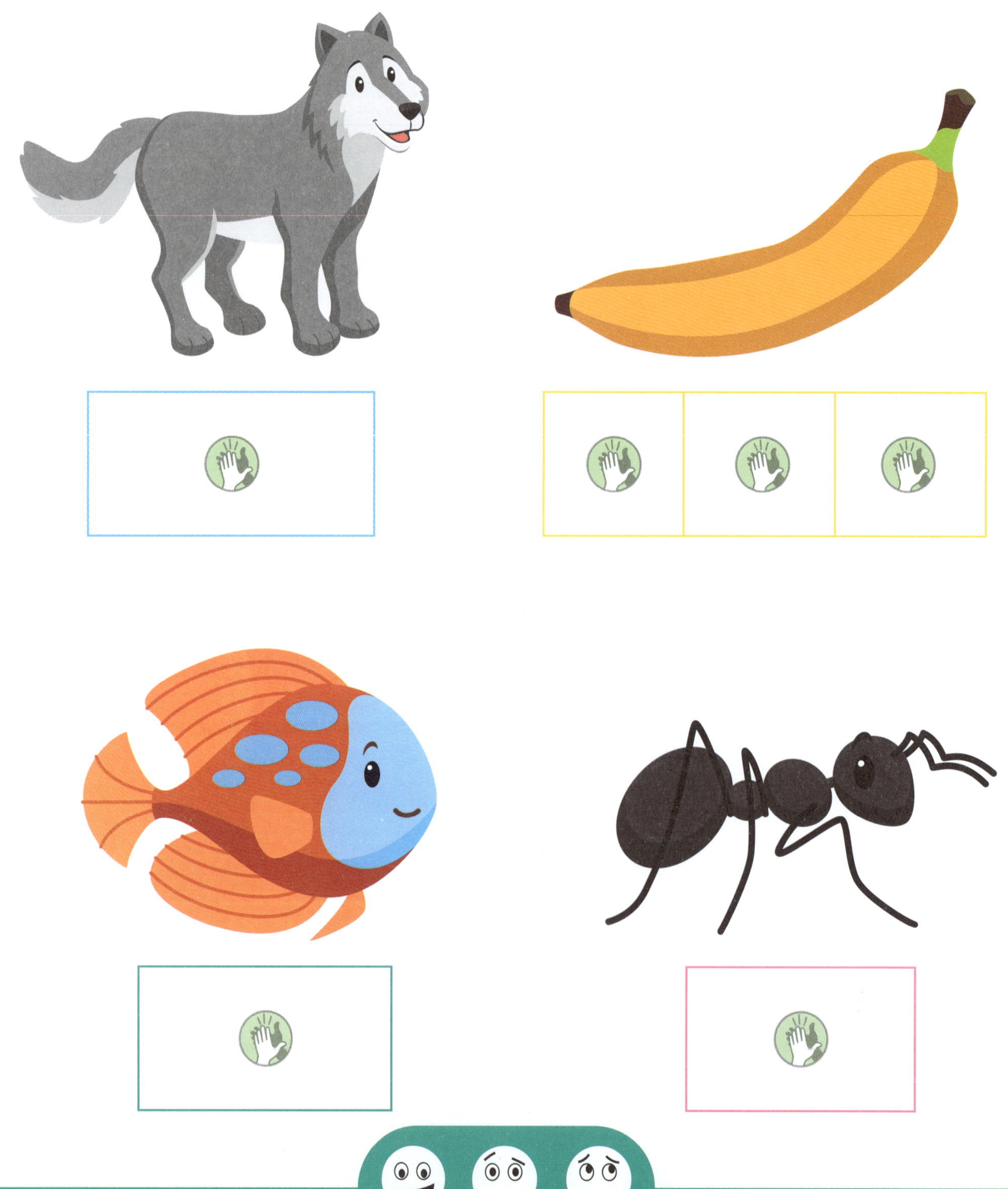

Got it! OK Not yet

CCSS.ELA-Literacy.RF.K.2.B

You need:

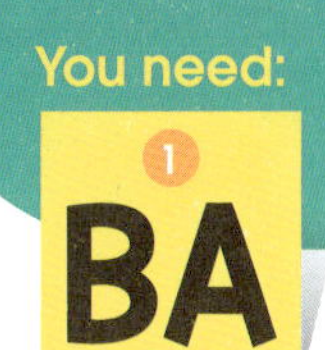

I can break apart the syllables in spoken words.

Cut out the pictures on the next page.
Say the name of each picture.
Clap and count each syllable.
Glue each picture on the backpack in the correct space.

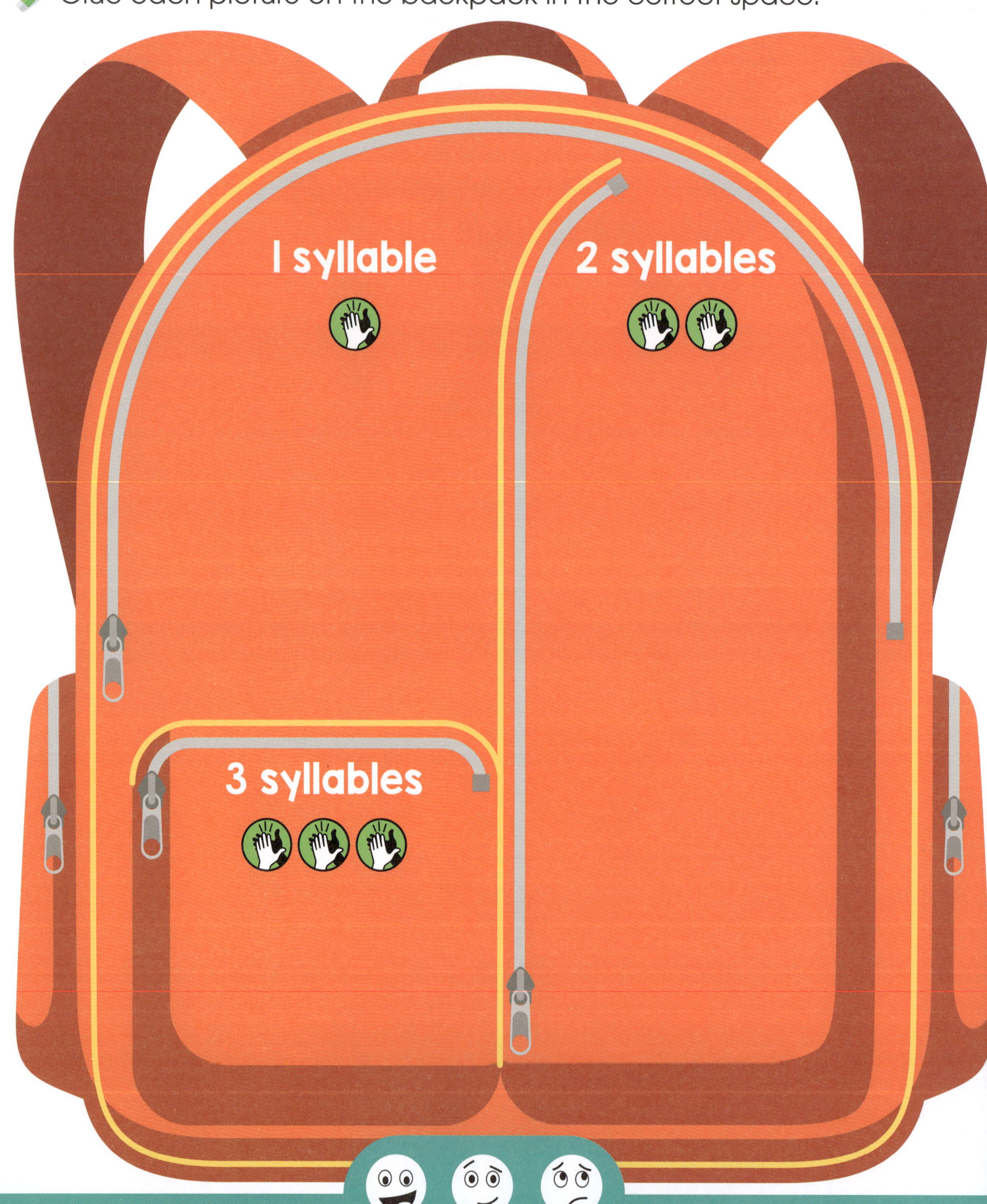

CCSS.ELA-Literacy.RF.K.2.B

You need:
GLUE

I can sort objects into categories to learn more about those categories.

 Draw a line from each picture to the place it belongs.

Got it!

OK

Not yet

You need:

I can sort objects into categories to learn more about those categories.

Draw a line from each picture to the place it belongs.

Got it!

OK

Not yet

CCSS.ELA-Literacy.L.K.5.A

I can sort objects into categories to learn more about those categories.

Draw a line from each picture to the bag it belongs in.

BASEBALL

HOCKEY

TENNIS

Got it! OK Not yet

I can find and say the beginning sound in a word.

 Circle the beginning sound for each picture.

 c d

 b r

 n m

 r u

 k s

 i l

 v w

 o c

 Got it!
 OK
 Not yet

CCSS.ELA-Literacy.RF.K.2.D

I can understand that the words I speak can be written with certain letters in a certain order.

Say the name of each picture.
Write **m** or **p** to begin each word.

___ig

___an

___ie

___om

Got it! OK Not yet

You need:

I can say the most common sound for each consonant.

Say the name of each picture.
Draw a line from each picture to its **beginning** letter.

Got it!

OK

Not yet

CCSS.ELA-Literacy.RF.K.3.A

You need:

I can say the most common sound for each consonant.

Say the name of each picture.
Draw a line from each picture to its **beginning** letter.

Got it!

OK

Not yet

I can say the most common sound for each consonant.

You need:

Say the name of each picture.
Draw a line from each picture to its **beginning** letter.

t

d

k

l

m

Got it!

OK

Not yet

CCSS.ELA-Literacy.RF.K.3.A

You need:

I can find and say the beginning sound in a word.

Circle the things in the picture that have the same beginning sound as .

Got it! OK Not yet

I can find and say the beginning sound in a word.

Cut out the pictures on the next page.
Say the name of each picture and sort it into the box with the same beginning sound.

b	c
s	d

Got it!  OK  Not yet

You need:

p

t

You need:

Let's have some fun.

Pick up each animal piece and make the sound each animal makes.

You need:

I can tell how words are different based upon the different sounds the letters make.

Draw a line from each word to the matching picture.

cat

bat

hat

Write the missing letter to make each word.

___at

___at

___at

Got it! OK Not yet

I can use matching or counting to compare groups of objects.

Which group has more objects?
Match the objects one to one.
Circle the number that is **greater**.
The first one is done for you.

5

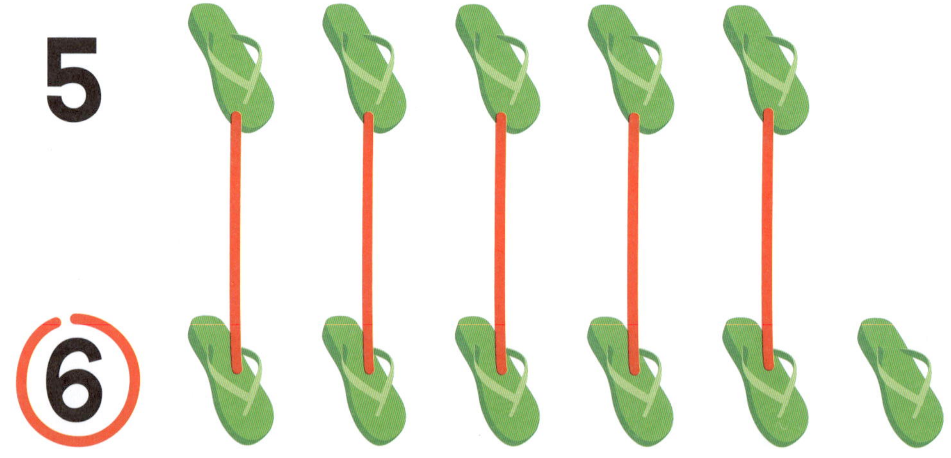

6

4

3

6

8

CCSS.Math.Content.K.CC.C.6

I can use matching or counting to compare groups of objects.

Greater means **more than**.

5 is **greater than 4.**

Count the number of birds on each branch.
Write the number in the box.
Circle the group that has **more** birds.

Got it!

OK

Not yet

You need:

I can use matching or counting to compare groups of objects.

Count the number of frogs on each log.
Write the number in the box.
Circle the group that has **more** frogs.

Got it!

OK

Not yet

CCSS.Math.Content.K.CC.C.6

You need:

I can use matching or counting to compare groups of objects.

Which group has fewer objects?
Match the objects one to one.
Circle the number that is **less**.
The first one is done for you.

2

4

5 

8 

7 

4 

Got it!

OK

Not yet

You need:

I can use matching or counting to compare groups of objects.

Less means **not as many**.

3 is **less than 5.**

Count the number of fish in each group.
Write the number in the box.
Circle the group that has **less** fish.

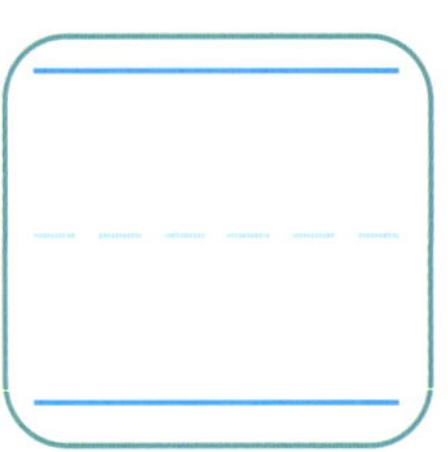
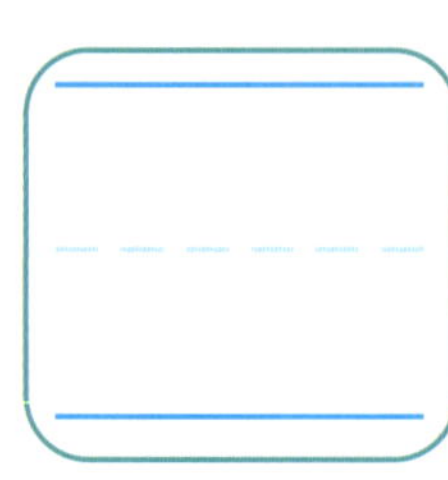

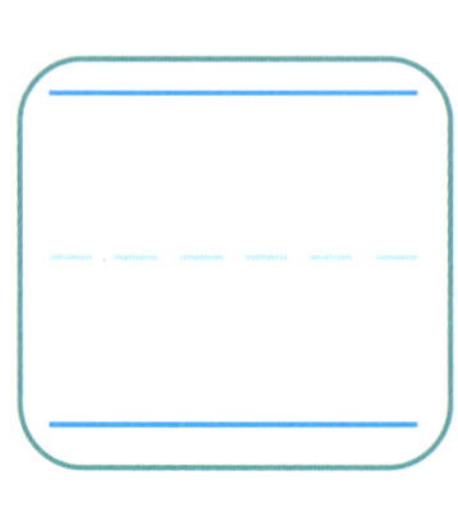

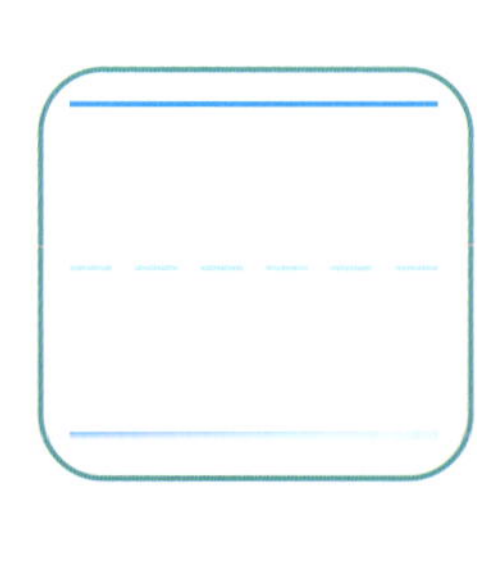

Got it! OK Not yet

CCSS.Math.Content.K.CC.C.6

You need:

I can use matching or counting to compare groups of objects.

Count the number of birds in each group.
Write the number in the box.
Circle the group that has **less** birds.

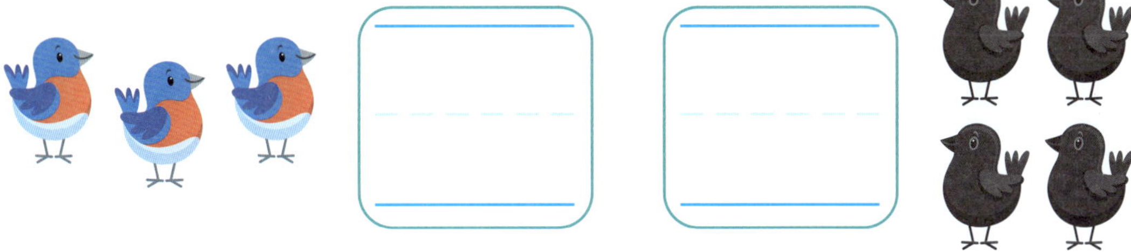

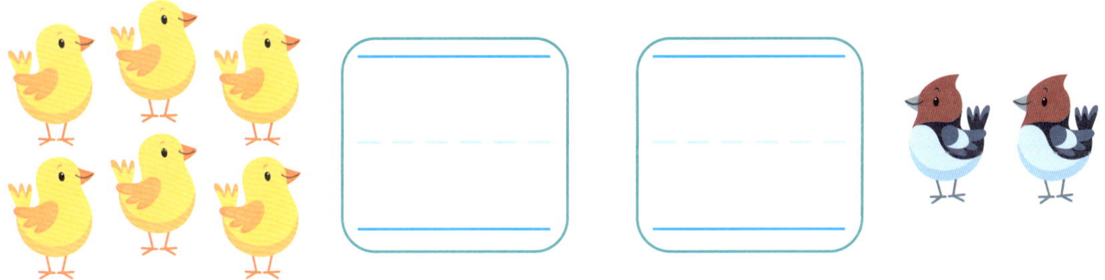

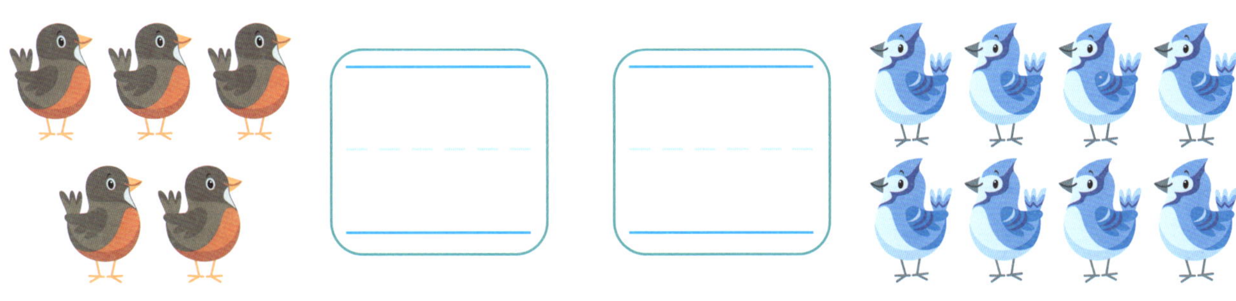

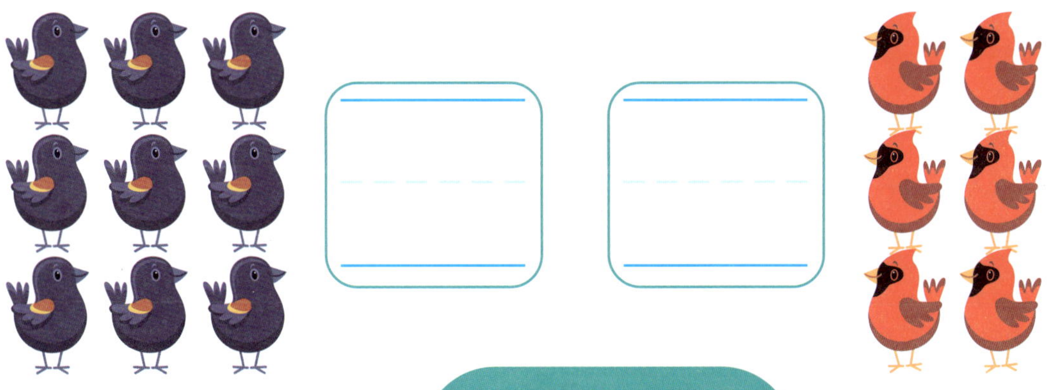

Got it! OK Not yet

I can use matching or counting to compare groups of objects.

Count each group.
Circle the group that has **1 less** than the first group in each row.

6

4

5

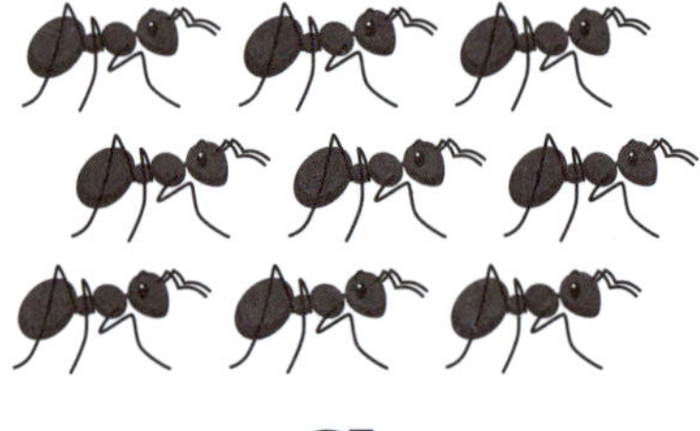

9

Got it!

OK

Not yet

CCSS.Math.Content.K.CC.C.6

I can name the author and illustrator of a nonfiction text with help.

You need:

✓ Check the front cover.

✗ Cross out the back cover.

Draw a line from **author** and **illustrator** to what each person did in the book.

Author	Illustrator

Parent Tip:
An illustrator is responsible for the artwork in a book. This can be pictures, diagrams, or photographs.

Got it!   OK   Not yet

You need:

I can explain how the pictures and words in a story work together in a nonfiction text with help.

Text Features
Things you notice in books that help you read and understand.

 Find and place the stickers onto the page.

This is a

bold word

close-up

Bears have a very good sense of smell.

label

caption

Got it! OK Not yet

CCSS.ELA-Literacy.RI.K.7

You need:

I can be an active learner in nonfiction reading activities.

Read the instructions.

Find a place that is **sunny**.
Dig a hole.
Set the tomato plant in the hole.
Pat dirt around the plant.
Water the plant often.
When the tomatoes are **ripe**,
eat and enjoy them!

 Circle the answers.

What does the word **sunny** mean?

What does the word **dig** mean?

What color are **ripe** tomatoes?

Got it!

OK

Not yet

I can answer questions about a new word in a story.

Read the story.

Ben has a pet hen.
The hen is red.
The hen lives in a pen.
The red hen lays eggs for Ben.
She lays one egg a day.

In this story what does the word **pen** mean?
Circle the answer.

pen

pen

Circle all of the things a hen can do in a pen.

Got it!

OK

Not yet

CCSS.ELA-Literacy.RL.K.4

I can compare two written numbers between 1 and 10.

Circle the answers.

How many [flower] are there? 4 5 6

How many [hummingbird] are there? 4 5 6

Which has **more**? [flower] [hummingbird]

How many [elephant] are there? 4 5 6

How many [giraffe] are there? 4 5 6

Which has **less**? [giraffe] [elephant]

Got it! OK Not yet

I can compare two written numbers between 1 and 10.

Who has two feet, four feet, more feet?
Count the number of feet on each animal and person.

How many have two feet? ________

How many have four feet? ________

Which are there **more** of?

Which are there **fewer** of?

CCSS.Math.Content.K.CC.C.7

You need:

Extra Credit!

Can you figure out how many feet live at your home? Count the feet of all of the people and animals that live with you. How many hands are there? Are there the same number of hands and feet?

Got it! OK Not yet

I can find and say the ending sound in a word.

 Circle the ending sound for each picture.

 s t

 y p

 g r

 m f

 t x

 b d

 Got it!
 OK
 Not yet

CCSS.ELA-Literacy.RF.K.2.D

I can find and say the ending sound in a word.

 Circle the ending sound for each picture.

v n

s r

g m

k h

k t

d b

Got it!

OK

Not yet

CCSS.ELA-Literacy.RF.K.2.D

I can understand that the words I speak can be written with certain letters in a certain order.

Say the name of each picture.
Write **m** or **n** to end each word.

su___

gu___

moo___

fa___

Got it!

OK

Not yet

CCSS.ELA-Literacy.RF.K.1.B

I can understand that the words I speak can be written with certain letters in a certain order.

Say the name of each picture.
Write **d** or **t** to end each word.

goa___

bir___

da___

boa___

Got it!

OK

Not yet

I can find and say the ending sound in a word.

Cut out the pictures on the next page.
Say the name of each picture and sort it into the box with the same ending sound.

t

n

m

d

Got it! OK Not yet

CCSS.ELA-Literacy.RF.K.2.D

You need:

p

l

Let's have some fun!

Draw a line through the maze from start to finish.

start

finish

You need: 13

I can count up to 20 to tell how many things are in a line, a box, or a circle.

Count each group of corn.
Find and place the number stickers 13 on the matching group.

Got it! OK Not yet

You need:

I can count up to 20 to tell how many things are in a line, a box, or a circle.

Read each number.
Color the beads to match the number.

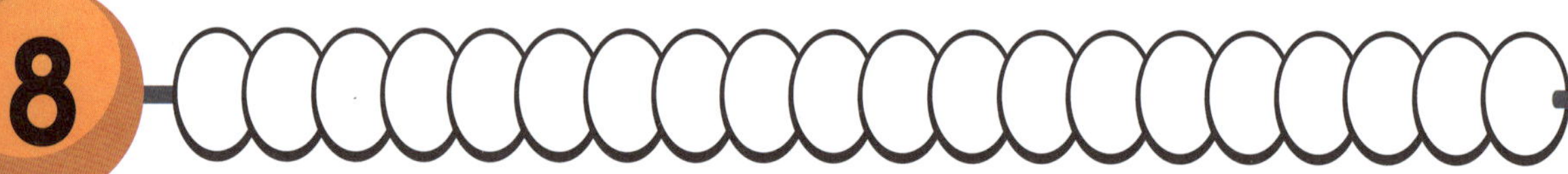

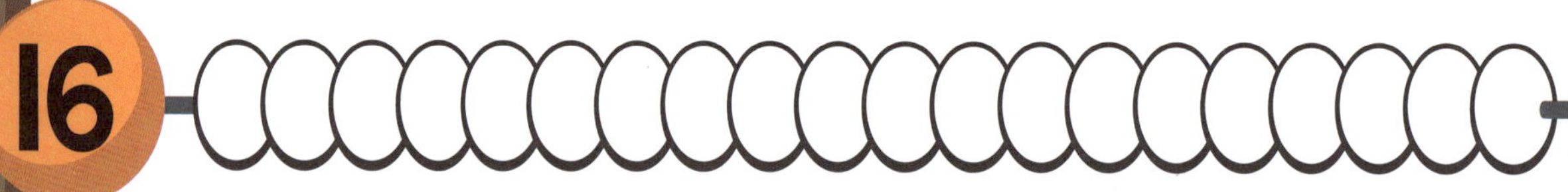

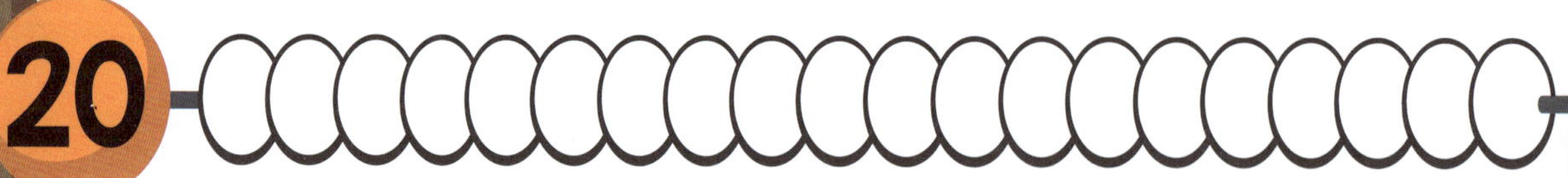

12

Got it!

OK

Not yet

CCSS.Math.Content.K.CC.B.5

I can count up to 20 to tell how many things are in a line, a box, or a circle.

Count each group.
Color the boxes to match the number.
Write the number.

Count	Color	Write

Got it! OK Not yet

I can count out a group of things when someone gives me any number from 1 to 20.

You need:

Find the press-out ant pieces and the spinner.

Spin the spinner and read the number the arrow lands on out loud.

Place that many on the picnic blanket.

Got it!

OK

Not yet

CCSS.Math.Content.K.CC.B.5

I can make the short and long vowel sounds for each of the five vowels.

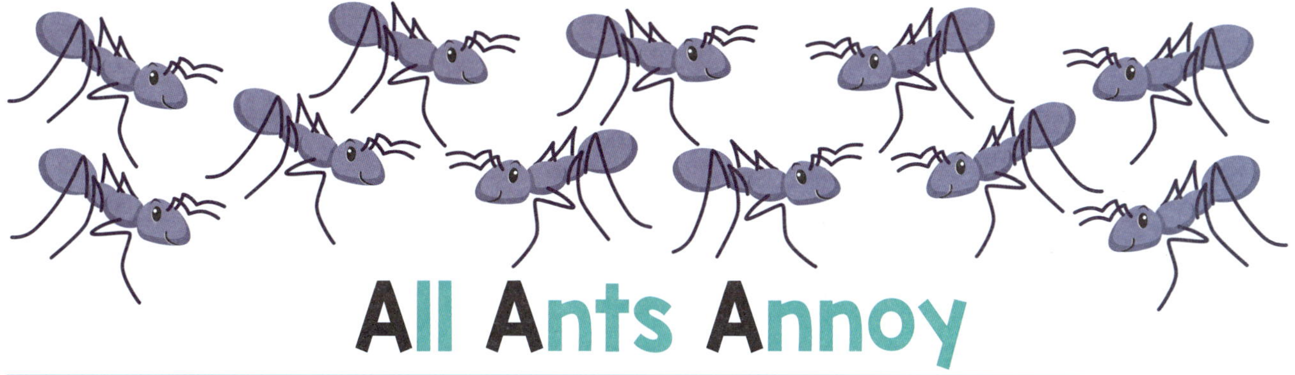

All Ants Annoy

 Draw a line to each picture that begins with the **short a** sound.

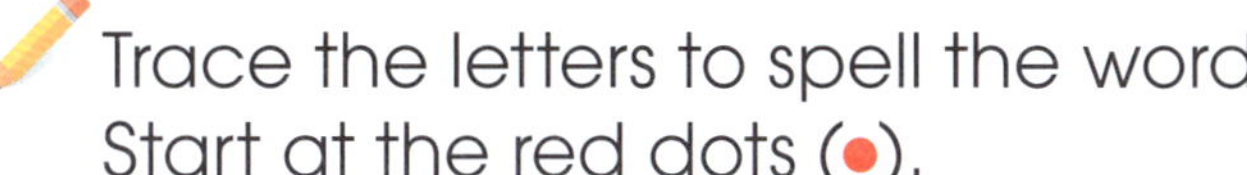 Trace the letters to spell the word.
Start at the red dots (●).

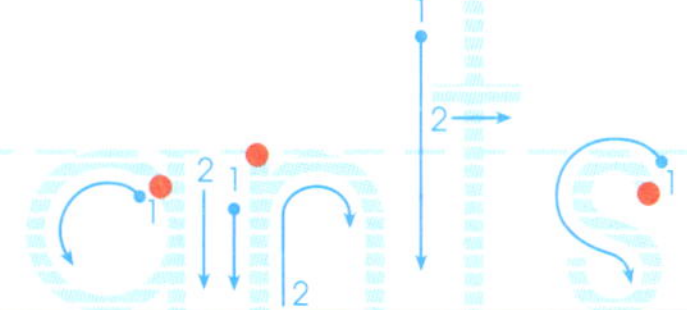

Got it!

OK

Not yet

You need:

I can make a short vowel sound for the letter a.

short a sound as in **apple**

Say the names of the pictures.

Write the letters to make **short a** words.

bat **cat** **fan** **pan**

Got it!

OK

Not yet

CCSS.ELA-Literacy.RF.K.3.B

You need:

I can make the short and long vowel sounds for each of the five vowels.

Eleven Elves Entertain

 Draw a line to each picture that begins with the **short e** sound.

 Trace the letters to spell the word.
Start at the red dots (●).

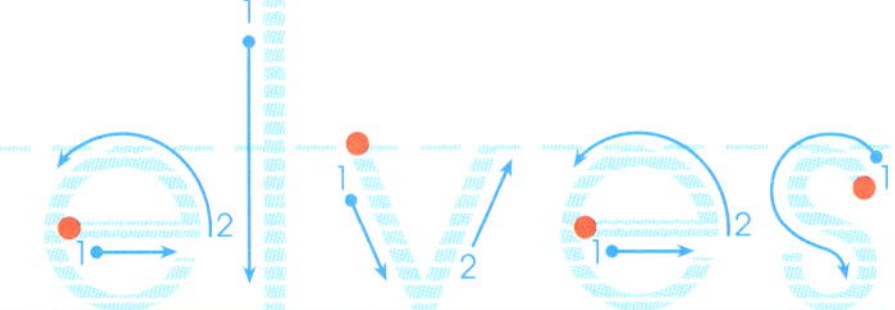

Got it!

OK

Not yet

I can make a short vowel sound for the letter e.

You need:

short e sound as in **nest**

Say the names of the pictures.

Write the letters to make **short e** words.

bed net pen web

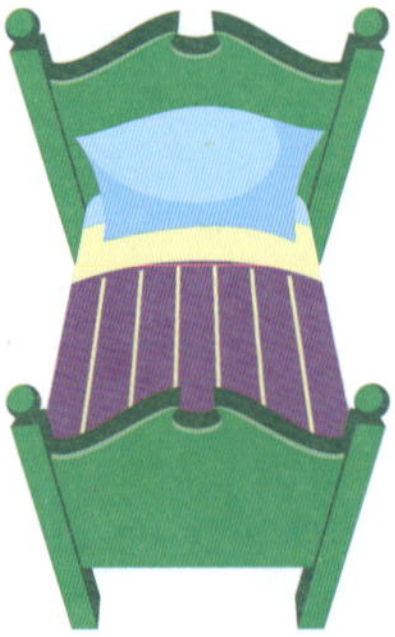

Got it! OK Not yet

CCSS.ELA-Literacy.RF.K.3.B

You need:

I can make the short and long vowel sounds for each of the five vowels.

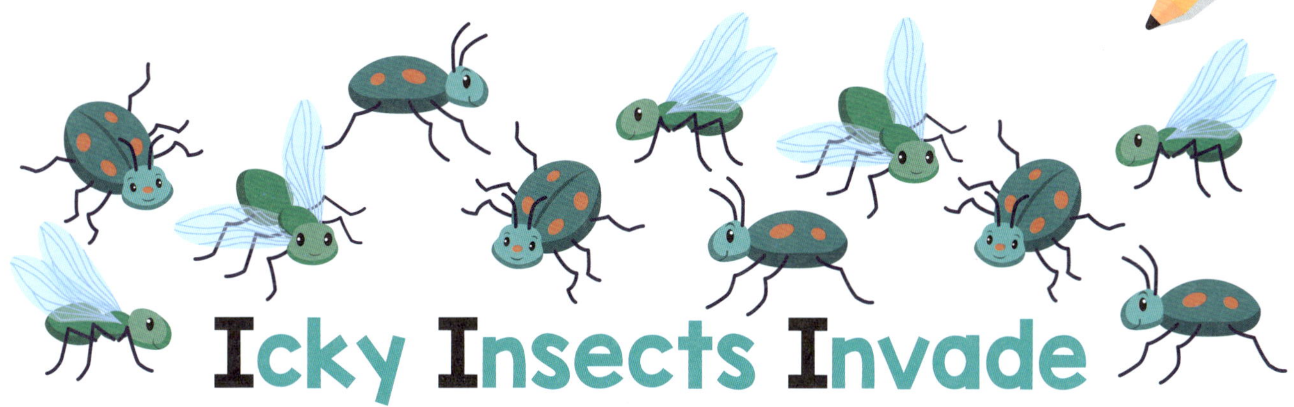

Icky Insects Invade

 Draw a line to each picture that begins with the **short i** sound.

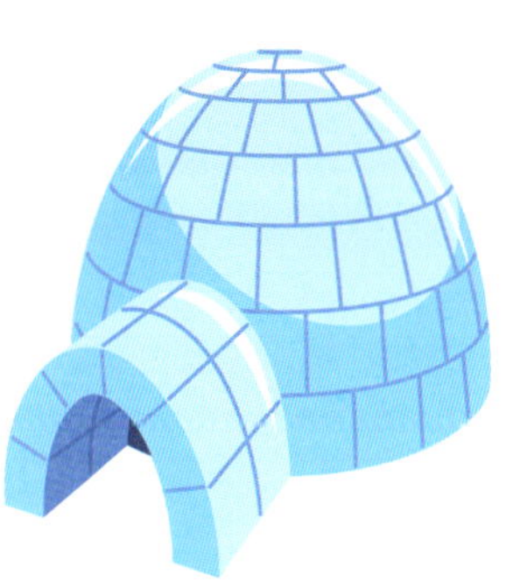

 Trace the letters to spell the word.
Start at the red dots (●).

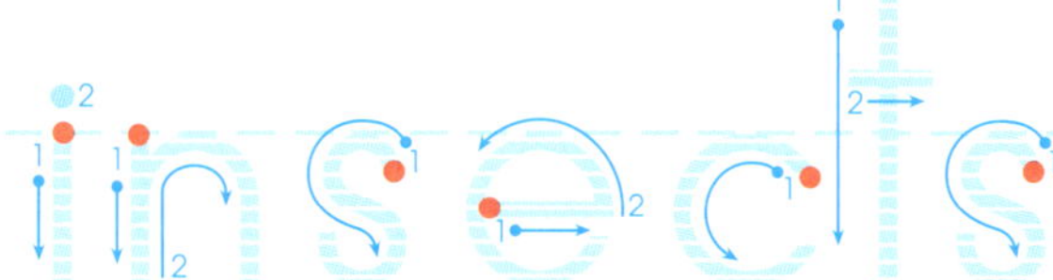

Got it!

OK

Not yet

I can make a short vowel sound for the letter i.

You need:

short i sound as in **igloo**

Say the names of the pictures.

 Write the letters to make **short i** words.

pig pin fin six

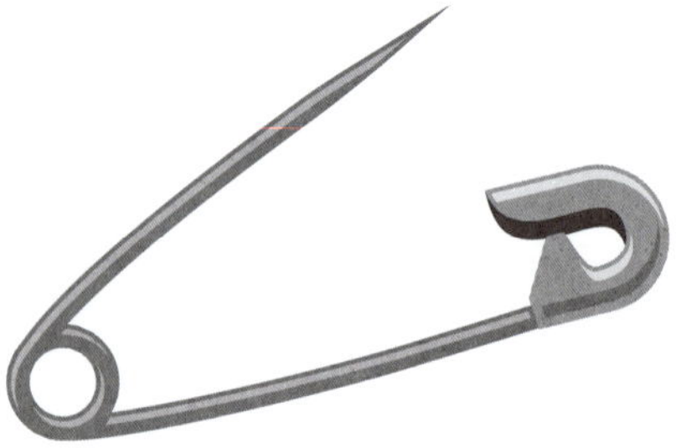

Got it! OK Not yet

CCSS.ELA-Literacy.RF.K.3.B

I can make the short and long vowel sounds for each of the five vowels.

You need:

Draw a line to each picture that begins with the **short o** sound.

Trace the letters to spell the word.
Start at the red dots (●).

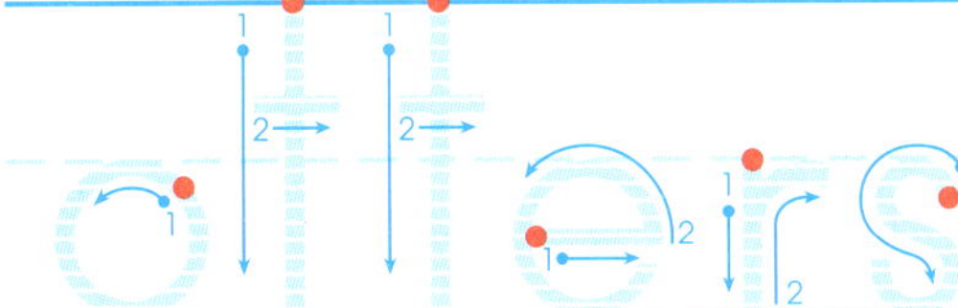

Got it!

OK

Not yet

I can make a short vowel sound for the letter o.

You need:

short o sound as in **octopus**

Say the names of the pictures.

Write the letters to make **short o** words.

pot **fox** **mop** **box**

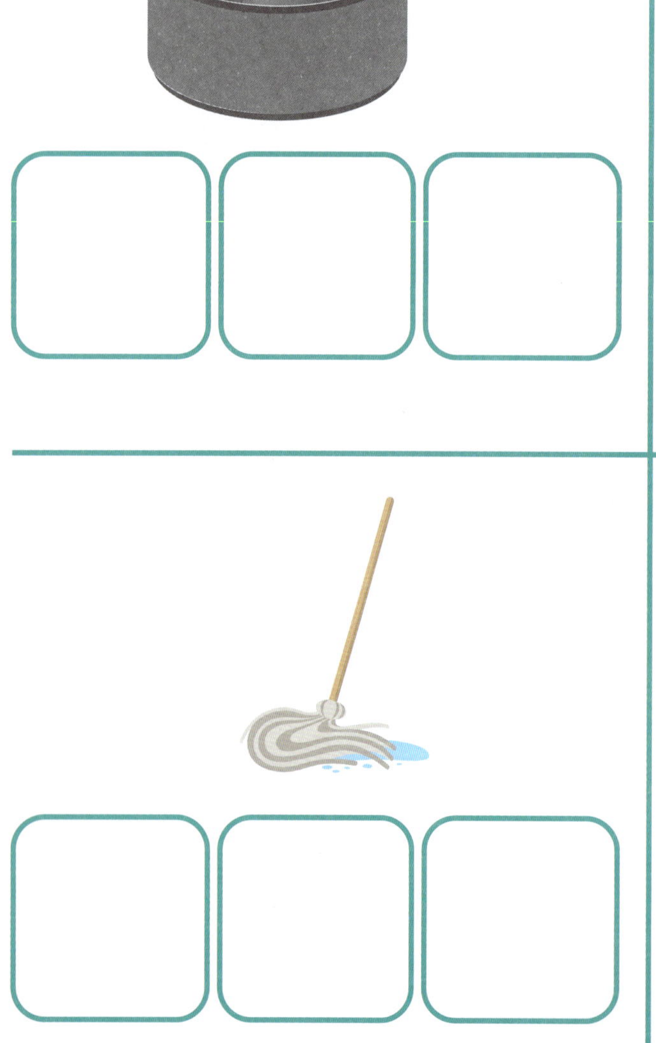

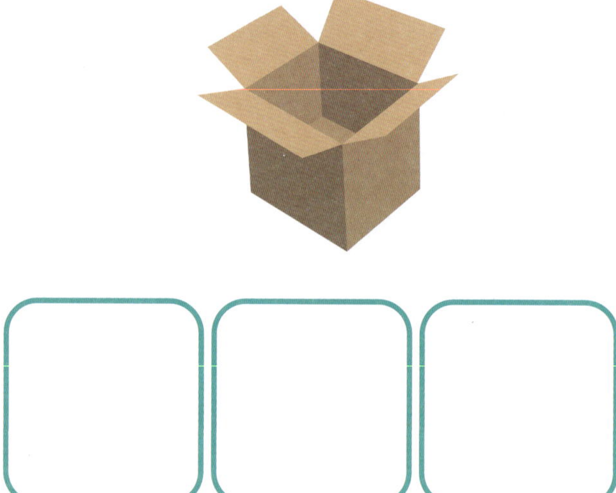

Got it!

OK

Not yet

CCSS.ELA-Literacy.RF.K.3.B

I can make the short and long vowel sounds for each of the five vowels.

Upbeat Umpires Understand

Draw a line to each picture that begins with the **short u** sound.

Trace the letters to spell the word.
Start at the red dots (•).

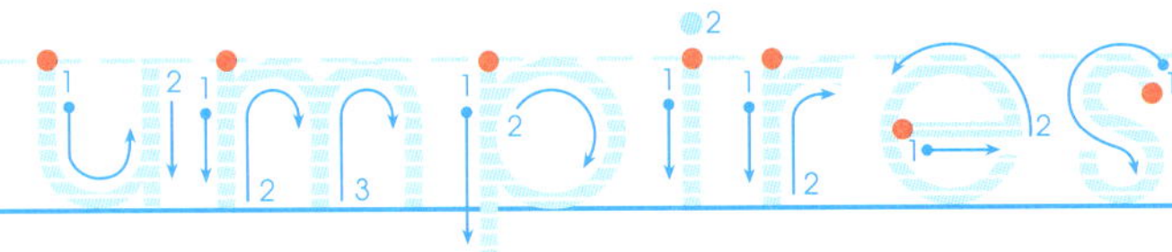

Got it!

OK

Not yet

I can make a short vowel sound for the letter u.

You need:

short u sound as in **umbrella**

Say the names of the pictures.

Write the letters to make **short u** words.

bus **cup** **sun** **bug**

Got it!

OK

Not yet

CCSS.ELA-Literacy.RF.K.3.B

I can make the short and long vowel sounds for each of the five vowels.

Say the name of each picture.
Circle the picture that has each **short vowel** sound.

Short a

Short e

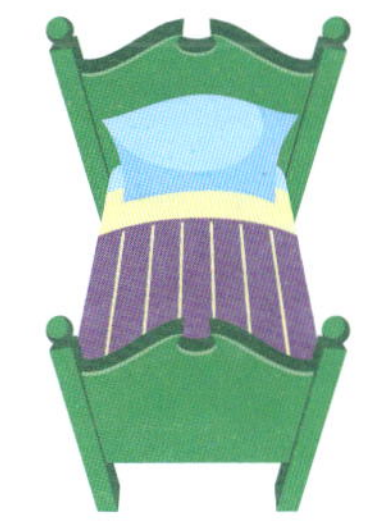

Short i

Short o

Short u

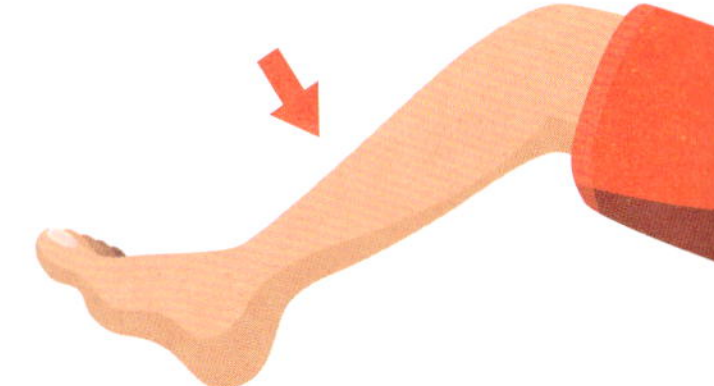

Got it!

OK

Not yet

I can make the short and long vowel sounds for each of the five vowels.

Say the name of each picture.
Circle the picture that has each **short vowel** sound.

Short a

Short e

 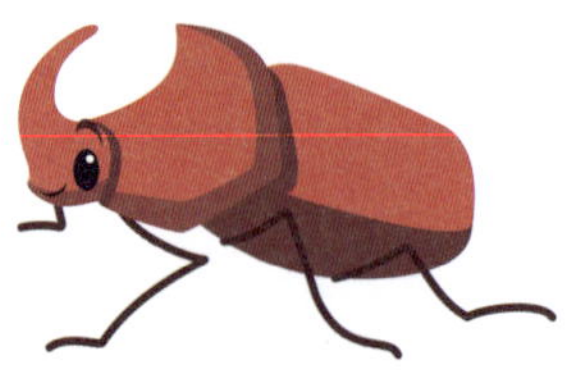 

Short i

Short o

Short u

Got it! OK Not yet

CCSS.ELA-Literacy.RF.K.3.B

I can show someone how I add or subtract by drawing pictures, using objects, using my fingers, or any other method.

You need:

How many are there **in all**?
Write the number.
The first one is done for you.

2  3  

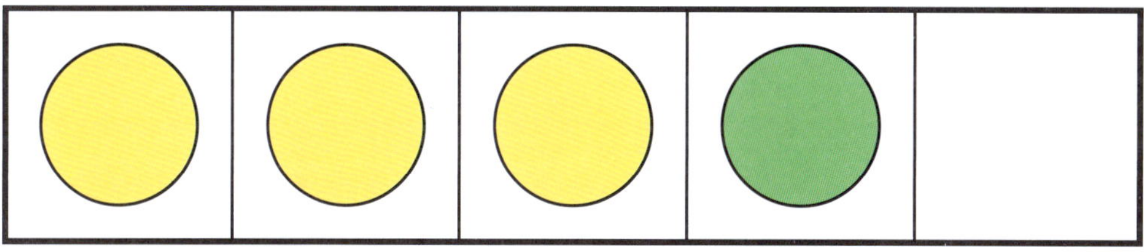

3  1 

1  2 

I can show someone how I add or subtract by drawing pictures, using objects, using my fingers, or any other method.

You need:

How many are there **altogether**?
Write the number.

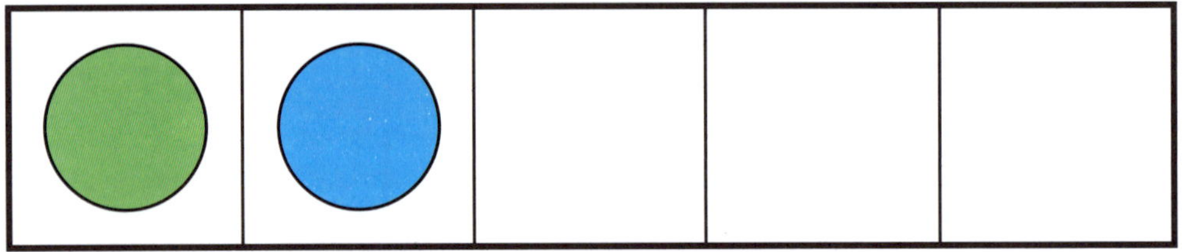

1 + 1 = ____

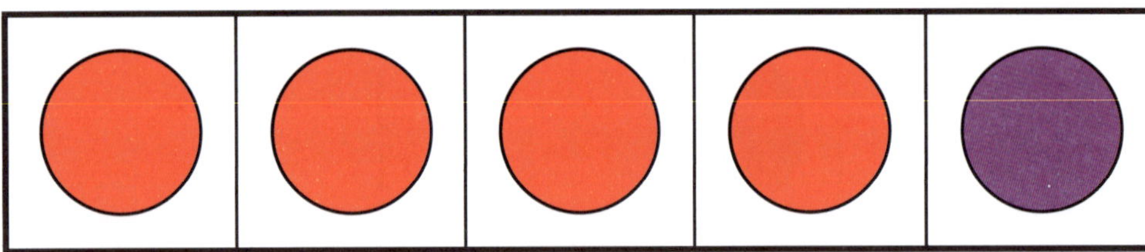

4 + 1 = ____

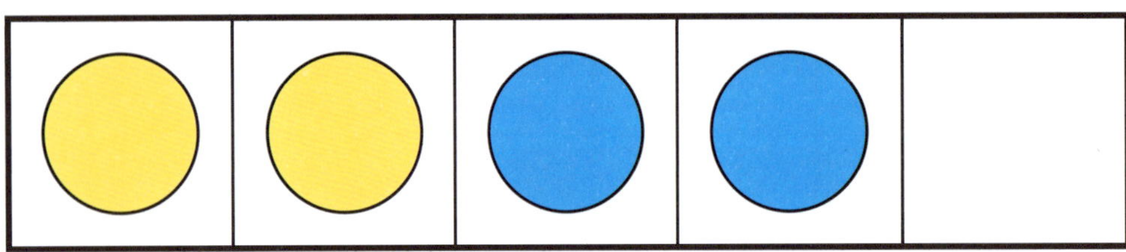

2 + 2 = ____

CCSS Math.Content.K.OA.A.1

I can show someone how I add or subtract by drawing pictures, using objects, using my fingers, or any other method.

You need:

How many are there **in all**?
Write the number.

Parent Tip:
If this is easy for your child, repeat these activities with objects such as pennies with answers up to 10.

6 + 3 = ____

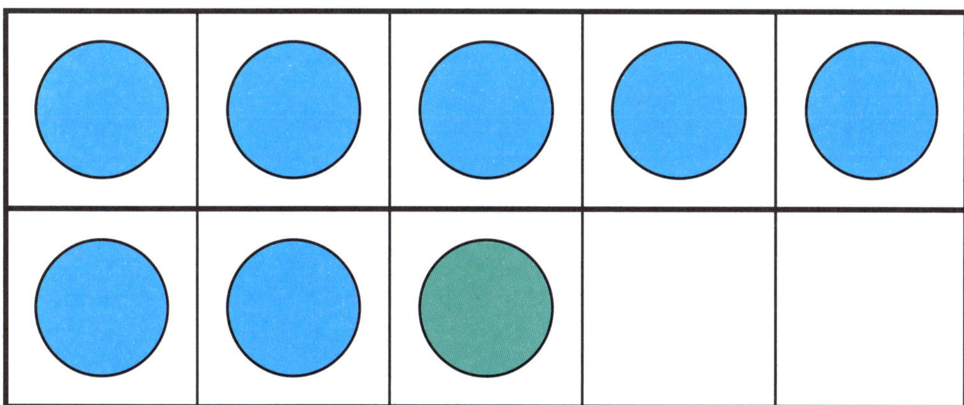

7 + 1 = ____

Got it! OK Not yet

I can show someone how I add or subtract by drawing pictures, using objects, using my fingers, or any other method.

You need:

How many are there **altogether**?
Write the number.

4 + 5 = ____

8 + 2 = ____

CCSS Math.Content.K.OA.A.1

You need:

I can understand that words are separated by spaces in print.

Find the **spaceman** press-out stick.

The spaceman helps you space the words in a sentence.

Place the spaceman between the words when you write.

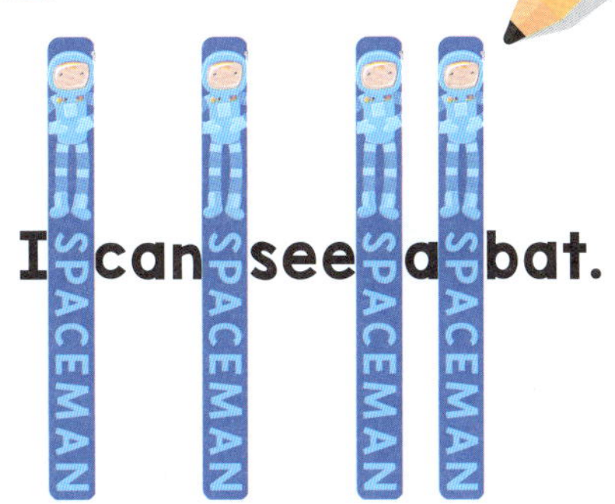

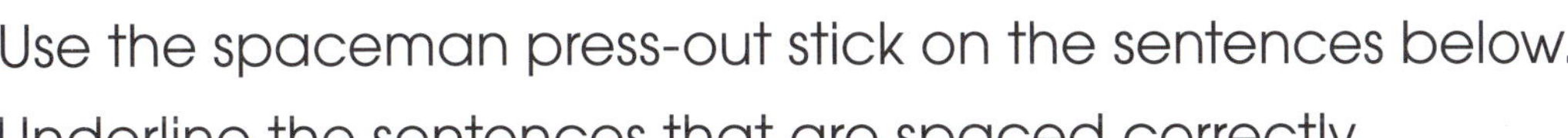

Use the spaceman press-out stick on the sentences below.

Underline the sentences that are spaced correctly.

Here is my dog.

Icanjump.

I can see the cat.

The tiger is big.

This is my fish.

I can understand that words are separated by spaces in print.

I like my bike.

Use the spaceman press-out stick to write the sentence below.

I like purple.

What is your favorite color?

Use the spaceman press-out stick to write the sentence below.

I like my bear.

What toy do you like?

CCSS.ELA-Literacy.RF.K.1.C

I can understand that words are separated by spaces in print.

Tap your finger on the ● under each word as you read the sentences.

I like dogs.

I am playing.

The hippo is big.

This is my cat.

I can see the bird.

Got it! OK Not yet

I can understand and use question words. (who, what, where, when, why, and how)

Parents: Review this story with your child.

Got it!

OK

Not yet

Who looks hungry?

Where is grandma's house?

What is in the basket?

How does the wolf feel at the end?

Got it! OK Not yet

I can answer the questions who, where, when, why, and how about a story with help.

You need:

Read the story.

Anna was in a bike race.
Anna looked down.
Her tire was flat.
Anna was sad.
She will try again.

Circle the answers.

Who is the story about?  **Jim**  **Anna**

When is the race?  **day**  **night**

Why did she not win?  **shoe**  **flat tire**

How did she feel at the end?  **sad**  **happy**

Got it!

OK

Not yet

CCSS.ELA-Literacy.RL.K.1

I can answer the questions who, where, when, why, and how about a story with help.

Read the story.

Scott was fishing.
Scott saw a fox on the rock.
The fox saw Scott.
The fox ran away.

Circle the answers.

Who is the story about?		Scott		Jill
Where is the fox sitting?		stump		rock
What did the fox do?		ran away		dug a hole
Why was Scott at the lake?	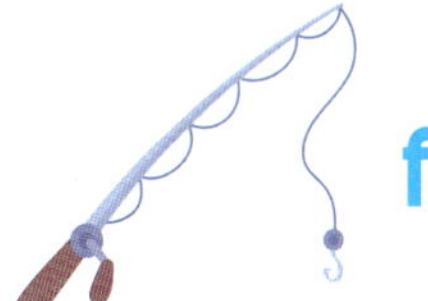	fishing		flying a kite

Got it!

OK

Not yet

I can answer the questions who, where, when, why, and how about a story with help.

 Circle the little picture that shows why this happened.

Got it!

OK

Not yet

CCSS.ELA-Literacy.RL.K.1

I can answer the questions who, where, when, why, and how about a story with help.

 Circle the little picture that shows why this happened.

Got it!

OK

Not yet

You need:

3

I can answer the questions who, where, when, why, and how about a story with help.

Find and place the 1 sticker on what happened **first**.

Find and place the 2 sticker on what happened **next**.

Find and place the 3 sticker on what happened **last**.

Got it! OK Not yet

CCSS.ELA-Literacy.RL.K.1

You need: 3

I can answer the questions who, where, when, why, and how about a story with help.

Find and place the 1 sticker on what happened **first**.
Find and place the 2 sticker on what happened **next**.
Find and place the 3 sticker on what happened **last**.

Got it!

OK

Not yet

CCSS.ELA-Literacy.RL.K.1

I can retell a story with help.

You need:

Cut out the story images on the next page.
Glue them in order and then tell the story out loud.

1	2	3
4	5	6

Got it!

OK

Not yet

CCSS.ELA-Literacy.RL.K.2

You need:

Got it!

OK

Not yet

You need:

I can show someone how I add or subtract by drawing pictures, using objects, using my fingers, or any other method.

How many are there **in all**?
Write the number.

2 + 2 = ____

3 + 2 = ____

1 + 2 = ____

4 + 2 = ____

Got it!

OK

Not yet

CCSS.Math.Content.K.OA.A.1

I can show someone how I add or subtract by drawing pictures, using objects, using my fingers, or any other method.

You need:

How many are there **altogether**?
Write the number.

1 + 4 = ____

5 + 2 = ____

3 + 3 = ____

7 + 1 = ____

Got it!

OK

Not yet

CCSS.Math.Content.K.OA.A.1

I can show someone how I add or subtract by drawing pictures, using objects, using my fingers, or any other method.

How many are there **in all**?
Write the number.

$0 + 3 =$ ____

$4 + 4 =$ ____

$5 + 1 =$ ____

$3 + 6 =$ ____

Got it! OK Not yet

You need:

I can show someone how I add or subtract by drawing pictures, using objects, using my fingers, or any other method.

How many are there **in all**?
Write the number.

8 + 1 = ____

6 + 2 = ____

6 + 0 = ____

5 + 4 = ____

Got it!

OK

Not yet

CCSS.Math.Content.K.OA.A.1

I can show someone how I add or subtract by drawing pictures, using objects, using my fingers, or any other method.

How many are there?
Circle the group that matches the number.

4 + 1 =

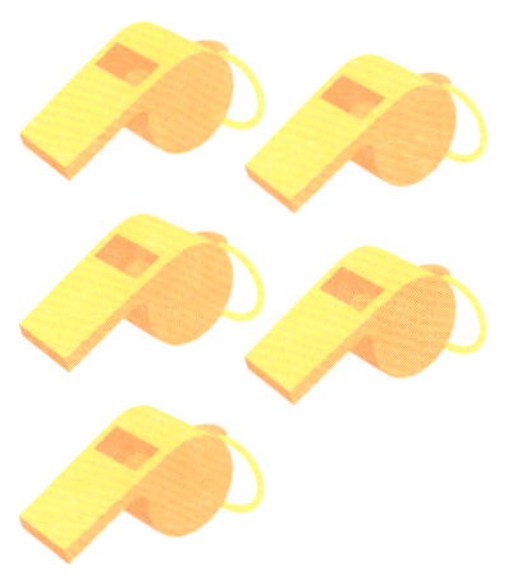

3 + 5 =

7 + 2 =

9 + 0 =

Got it!

OK

Not yet

CCSS.Math.Content.K.OA.A.1

You need:

I can understand and name end punctuation or end marks.

A **statement** is a sentence that starts with an uppercase letter and ends with a **period** (.).

Here is my shoe.

Write a **period** at the end of each sentence.

The dog is big.

Our cat is little

I am happy

I like fish

You need:

I can understand and name end punctuation or end marks.

A **question** is a sentence that starts with an uppercase letter and ends with a **question mark** (**?**).
A question asks **who**, **what**, **when**, **where**, **why**, and **how**.

Where is my shoe?

Write a **question mark** at the end of each sentence.

How are you?

When is lunch

What is this

Who is that

Got it! OK Not yet

I can understand and name end punctuation or end marks.

An **exclamation** is a sentence that starts with an uppercase letter and ends with an **exclamation point** (!). An exclamation point is used to express strong emotions.

I am so excited to see you!

Write an **exclamation point** at the end of each sentence.

I am mad !

Look at that

It was fun

Circle the face showing a strong emotion.

Got it!

OK

Not yet

CCSS.ELA-Literacy.L.K.2.B

I can understand and name end punctuation or end marks.

Cut out the ! shapes.

! Place a punctuation mark at the end of each line and read the word or phrase as a **statement**, **question**, or **exclamation**.

Look at the book

Look out

I am mad

Can I play

Did you like it

! ? . ? !

Got it!

OK

Not yet

I can read common words.

You need:

Find and circle the words in the list below.
Words are only going across.

THE	YOU	FOR	LITTLE
AND	SAID	LOOK	DOWN

W R F Y O U P U Y R
T I N A N D K X K V
U T Z R W M Y P U F
M G B U R B J X X J
T H E O A W L O O K
I G M T T B J U G T
R F Q S A I D O W N
A Z J M W K C O H N
L I T T L E B P B G
Z E D F O R X H J C

Got it!  OK  Not yet

CCSS.ELA-Literacy.RF.K.3.C

I can read common words.

Read the poem below.

Circle the word **little**.

Underline the word **the**.

Look at the little bug.

It likes to run on the big blue rug.

"Watch out, little bug!" said the boy.

"Or I will run you down with my toy."

Got it! OK Not yet

I can say regular plural nouns.

Write a **s** at the end of each word to make it plural.
Draw a line from the word to the matching picture.
The first one is done for you.

6 can s

2 boy

5 tree

3 cat

4 girl

Got it! OK Not yet

CCSS.ELA-Literacy.L.K.1.C

I can say regular plural nouns.

Cut out the booklet pages below and fold along the center line. Combine these pages with the booklet pages from page 105 to make a book. Then read the book out loud.

COUNT
WITH ME

Fold along this line.

one

two

three

four

five

I have
1 ball.

I love
my toys!

I can say regular plural nouns.

Cut out the booklet pages below and fold along the center line. Combine these pages with the booklet pages from page 103 to make a book. Then read the book out loud.

I have 2 skates.

Fold along this line.

I have 5 dolls.

I have
3 cars.

I have
4 blocks.

You need:

I can read common words.

Find and circle the words in the list below.
Words are only going across.

CAN	NOT	BIG	WHERE
SEE	ONE	COME	JUMP

C	O	M	E	X	L	T	K	G	W
N	V	O	Q	E	Q	B	I	G	M
J	N	I	D	W	H	E	R	E	D
D	O	Y	V	S	N	J	E	N	Y
I	M	W	Y	I	W	K	X	F	H
J	U	M	P	U	J	I	C	A	N
W	V	J	C	N	H	N	G	H	V
S	O	O	N	E	T	L	S	E	E
E	Q	X	E	V	W	Q	M	A	T
R	C	J	N	O	T	Z	B	B	G

Got it!

OK

Not yet

You need:

I can read common words.

Draw a line from each word to the matching picture. The first one is done for you.

little

up

big

down

Got it!

OK

Not yet

CCSS.ELA-Literacy.RF.K.3.C

I can blend and divide onsets and rimes of single syllable words.

Read the story below.

Cut out the green letters r.

Glue the letters r into the ☐ to finish the words in the story.

The ☐at is small.

So is the ☐at.

The ☐at is tall.

t
b
w
r
b
c

Got it! OK Not yet

You need:

I can blend and divide onsets and rimes of single syllable words.

Read the story below.

Cut out the **orange** letters t on the previous page.

Glue the letters t into the ☐ to finish the words in the story.

The ☐all girl

had a ☐all.

She kicked it

over the ☐all.

Got it! OK Not yet

CCSS.ELA-Literacy.RF.K.2.C

You need:

I can show someone how I add or subtract by drawing pictures, using objects, using my fingers, or any other method.

You can write an **addition number sentence** like this: **1 + 2 = 3**

Write the addition number sentences.

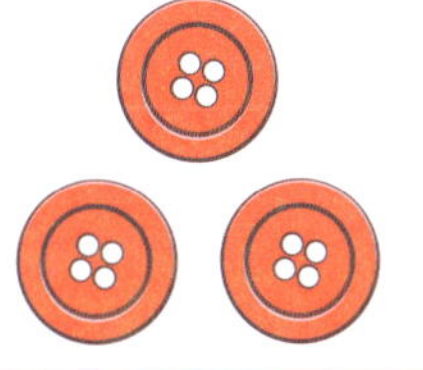

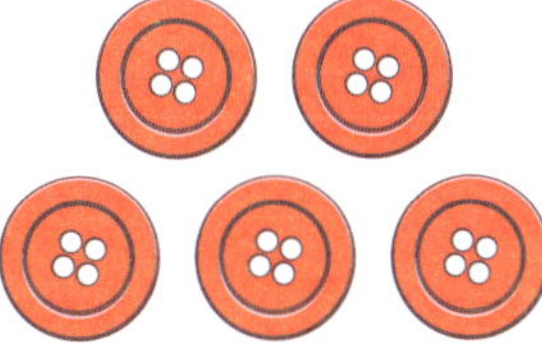

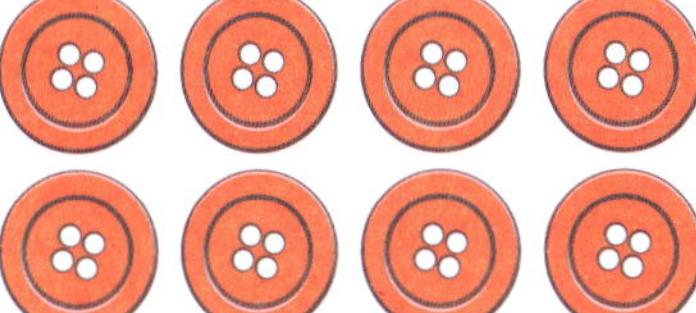

Try It!

You can do finger addition. Hold up three fingers on one hand. Now hold up three on the other. How many fingers are up? Try this again with a different number of fingers.

Got it!

OK

Not yet

I can use objects or drawings to solve addition word problems up to 10.

Read the word problems.
Write the addition number sentences.

Katie picked **2** carrots.
Then she picked **2 more**.
How many did she pick **in all**?

____ + ____ = ____

Ethan can see **5** birds on the fence.
Then **3 more** birds came.
How many birds are there on the fence **in all**?

____ + ____ = ____

Got it! OK Not yet

CCSS.Math.Content.K.OA.A.2

I can add numbers within 5.

You need:

Write your answers.

2 + 1 = ____

1 + 0 = ____

1 + 4 = ____

4 + 0 = ____

3 + 1 = ____

2 + 3 = ____

3 + 0 = ____

1 + 2 = ____

3 + 2 = ____

2 + 2 = ____

1 + 1 = ____

GOAL! Try to get 10 correct in **1 minute.**

I can add numbers within 5.

You need:

Write your answers.

1 + 1 = ____

2 + 3 = ____

3 + 0 = ____

4 + 1 = ____

1 + 3 = ____

3 + 2 = ____

3 + 1 = ____

1 + 4 = ____

4 + 0 = ____

1 + 2 = ____

2 + 2 = ____

5 + 0 = ____

Got it!

OK

Not yet

CCSS.Math.Content.K.OA.A.5

I can count to 50 by ones and tens.

Count to **50**.
Write the missing numbers.
Circle the numbers **10**, **20**, **30**, **40**, and **50**.

1		3				7			10
	12		14		16			19	
		23	24				28		30
31	32			35				39	
			44			47			

Not yet

I can tell the characters, settings, and important events in a story with help.

You need:

Read the book **The New Bike**.

Circle all of the characters in the book **The New Bike**.

Circle the setting where the story took place.

Check what happened first in the book.

Got it!

OK

Not yet

CCSS.ELA-Literacy.RL.K.3

I can read and understand kindergarten books.

You need:

Parents:
Please read the book **The New Bike** to your child. Then ask the following questions.

Why did the author write this book?

To tell a story about a girl and her bike.

To teach you how to brake.

How does Lee feel when she imagines showing her bike to Mike?

happy

sad

Who helps Lee learn to ride her bike?

mom

dad

Look at the picture.
Is Lee mad when she falls off her bike?

yes **no**

Did you like reading **The New Bike**?

yes **no**

Parent Tip:
Go to SchoolZone.com and find other Start to Read!® books like **The New Bike** and **Underwater**.

I can explain how two characters have similar and different experiences with help.

You need: 

Read the two stories below.

Anna's Race

Anna and Ted were in a bike race.
Anna's bike had a flat tire.
Anna was not mad.
She will try another time.

Ted's Race

Ted was in a bike race.
Ted's bike had a flat tire.
Ted was angry.
He cried and went home.

Circle  **true** or  **false**.

Anna and Ted were in a bike race.  

Anna had a flat tire.  

Ted went home.  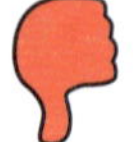

Ted won the race.  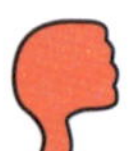

Ted was happy.  

Anna was mad.  

Got it!

OK

Not yet

CCSS.ELA-Literacy.RL.K.9

I can write, draw, and tell my readers what topic I am writing about and then tell them my opinion.

Opinions tell someone what you think.

Megan wrote an opinion on her favorite book.

What is your favorite book?

My favorite book is Charlie Hides.

I like it because it is funny.

Got it!

OK

Not yet

I can write, draw, and tell my readers what topic I am writing about and then tell them my opinion.

In an **opinion** you use the word *because* to explain your thinking.

Faye wrote an opinion on her favorite pet.

My favorite pet is a cat.

I like cats because they are playful and they purr.

What is Faye's favorite pet? **dogs** **cats** **birds**

Why does Faye like them? **they are big** **they are playful**

CCSS.ELA-Literacy.W.K.3

I can write, draw, and tell my readers what topic I am writing about and then tell them my opinion.

What is your favorite dessert?

Circle the answer, and then finish the sentence.

My favorite dessert is ______.

It is my favorite dessert because ______

______.

Got it! OK Not yet

I can write, draw, and tell my readers what topic I am writing about and then tell them my opinion.

What is your favorite thing to do?

Finish the sentences.

My favorite thing to do is ______________________________.

It is my favorite thing to do because ______________________________.

Got it! OK Not yet

CCSS.ELA-Literacy.W.K.3

I can write, draw, and tell my readers what topic I am writing about and then tell them my opinion.

Write an **opinion** about something you like.
Remember to use the word "because."

I like

Draw a picture to go along with what you wrote.

Writing Checklist:

- [ ] I added a picture with details.
- [ ] I used the word "because."
- [ ] I used a capital letter at the beginning of each sentence.
- [ ] I used a (.) or (!) at the end of each sentence.

Got it! OK Not yet

Let's have some fun!

You need: 

 Color the scene.

1 =  2 = 3 = 4 = 5 =

6 = 7 =

Got it! OK Not yet

I can read and understand kindergarten books.

Cut out the booklet pages below and fold along the center line. Combine these pages with the booklet pages from page 127 to make a book. Then read the book out loud.

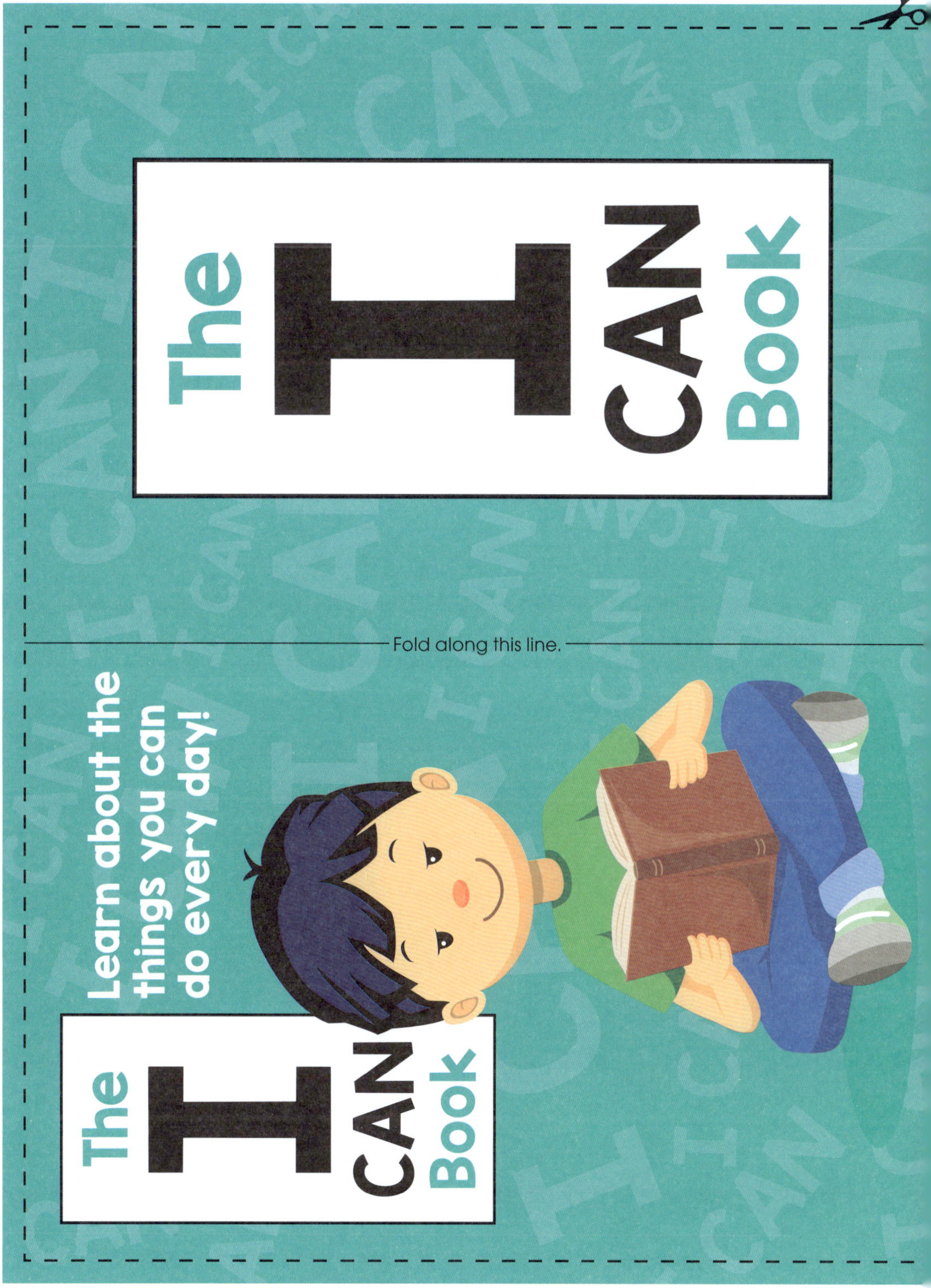

The I CAN Book

Fold along this line.

The I CAN Book

Learn about the things you can do every day!

I can see.

I can help.

I can read and understand kindergarten books.

Cut out the booklet pages below and fold along the center line. Combine these pages with the booklet pages from page 125 to make a book. Then read the book out loud.

Fold along this line.

I can eat.

I can read.

I can correctly name shapes even when their sizes and positions are different.

A **circle** is a shape that looks like this: 

How many ○ can you find? ____________

Got it! OK Not yet

You need:

I can correctly name shapes even when their sizes and positions are different.

A **diamond** is a shape that looks like this:

How many ◇ can you find? ______________

Got it! OK Not yet

I can correctly name shapes even when their sizes and positions are different.

An **oval** is a shape that looks like this: 

How many  ⬭ can you find? ______________

Got it! OK Not yet

I can correctly name shapes even when their sizes and positions are different.

You need:

Find and circle the hidden ◯ **circles**, ◇ **diamonds**, and ⬭ **ovals**.

Got it! OK Not yet

CCSS.Math.Content.K.G.A.2

You need:

I can write a letter or letters for most consonant and short vowel sounds.

C and **h** work together to make a new sound like the word **cherry** .

Jaz is trying to find **ch** sounds.

Draw lines from pictures that start with **ch** to Jaz.

chess

cow

check

banana

fish

bird

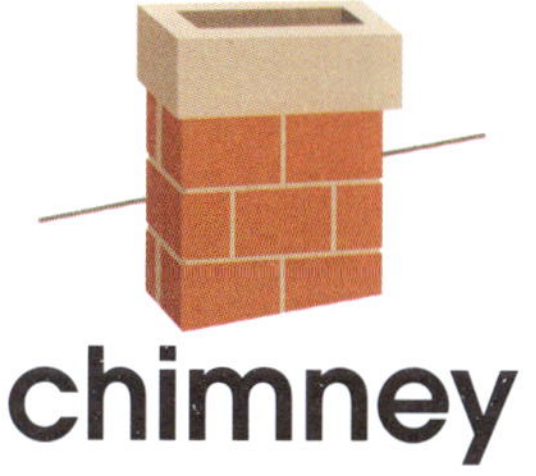
chimney

chocolate

glass

cherry

Got it!

OK

Not yet

I can write a letter or letters for most consonant and short vowel sounds.

T and **h** work together to make a new sound like the word **thumb**.

Color the pictures that start with **th**.

thunder

chair

thumb

horn

thread

horse

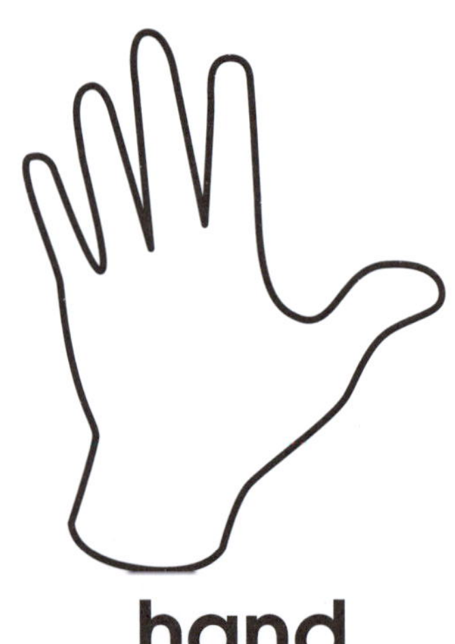
hand

house

thirty

Got it!

OK

Not yet

CCSS.ELA-Literacy.L.K.2.C

You need:

I can write a letter or letters for most consonant and short vowel sounds.

Write the letters **bl** to start each word.

______ood

______ock

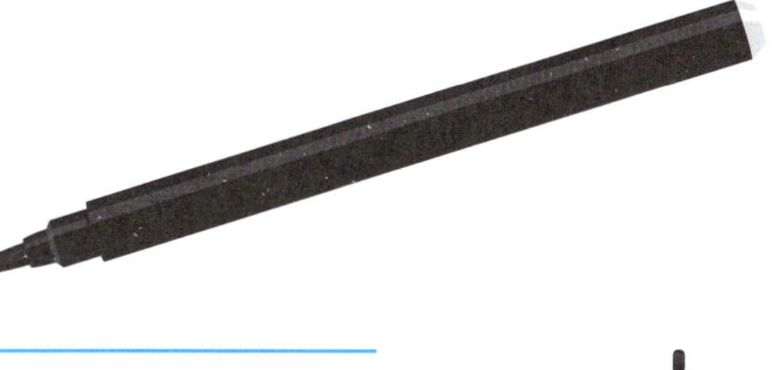

______ack

Write the letters **cl** to start each word.

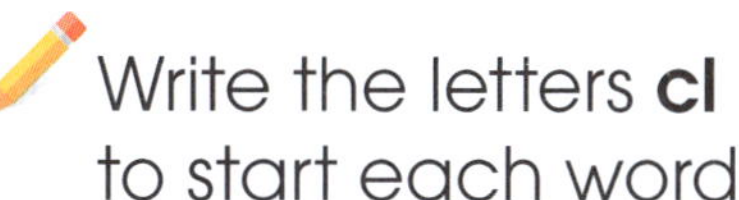

______ock

______oud

______ap

Got it!

OK

Not yet

I can write a letter or letters for most consonant and short vowel sounds.

S and **h** work together to make a new sound like the word **shovel**.

Write the letters **sh** to start each word.

Color the pictures.

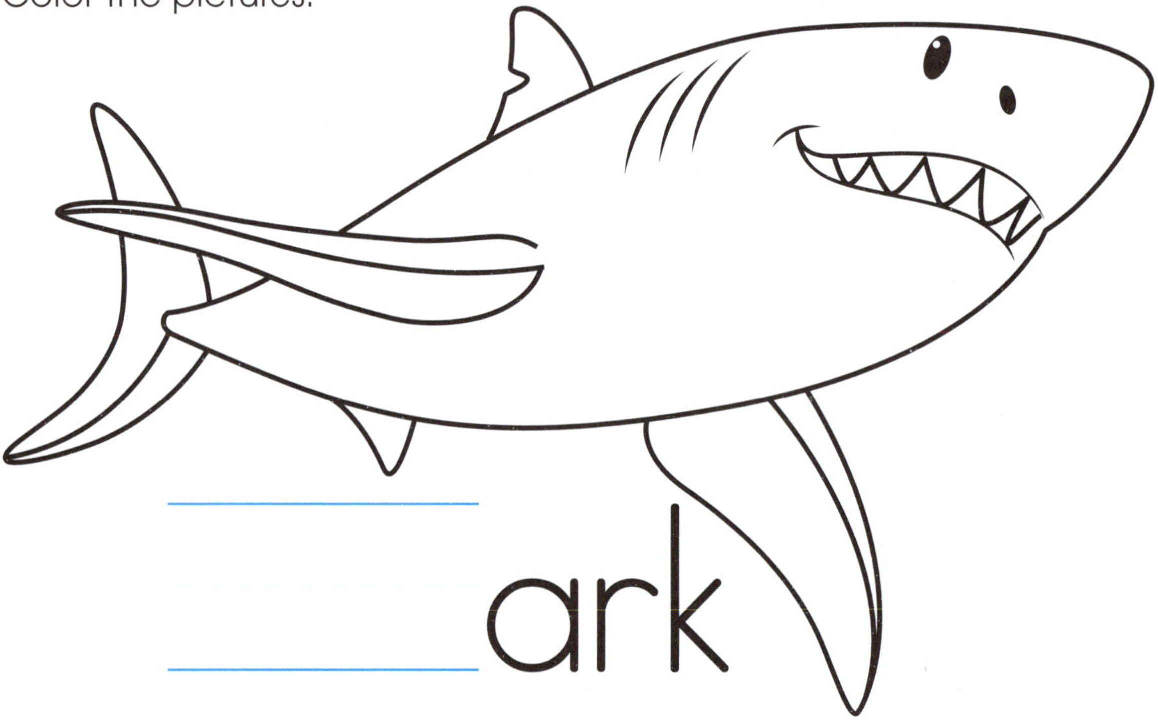

______ark

______ip

______ell

Got it! OK Not yet

I can write a letter or letters for most consonant and short vowel sounds.

P and **l** work together to make a new sound like the word **plum** .

Write the letters **pl** to start each word.

Color the pictures.

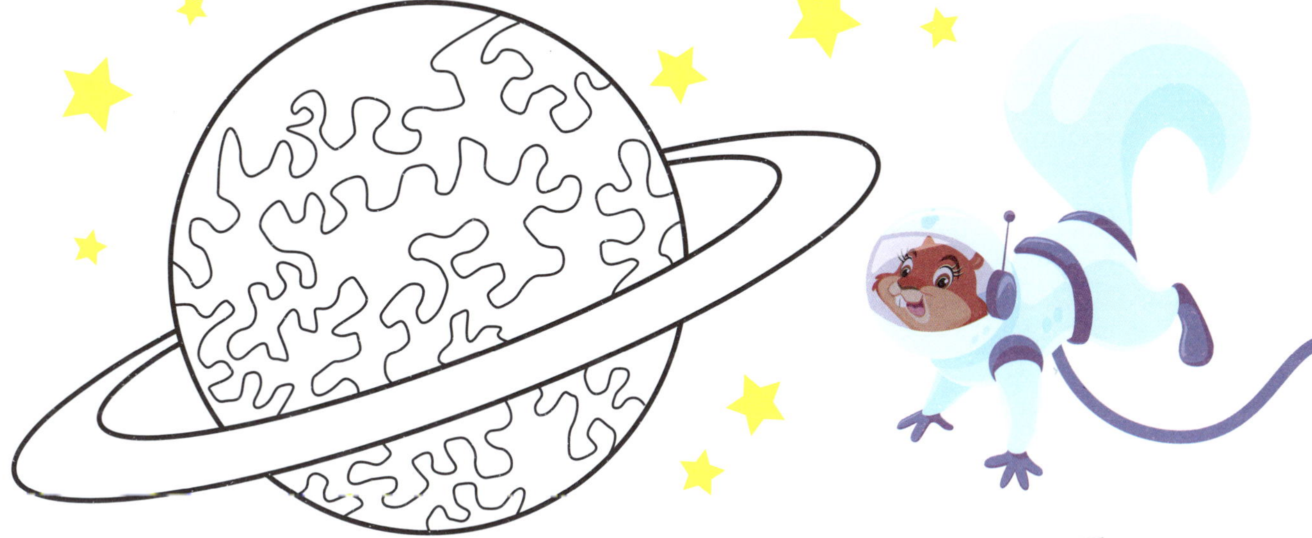

_____anet

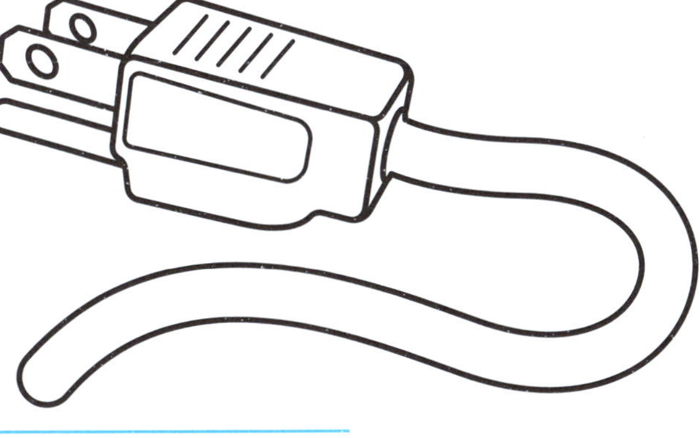

_____ug

_____ant

Got it! OK Not yet

You need:

I can write a letter or letters for most consonant and short vowel sounds.

Write the letters **fl** to start each word.

Say each word.

Color the pictures.

ag

CCSS.ELA-Literacy.L.K.2.C

I can write a letter or letters for most consonant and short vowel sounds.

Write the letters **sl** to start each word.

Say each word.

Color the pictures.

_____oth

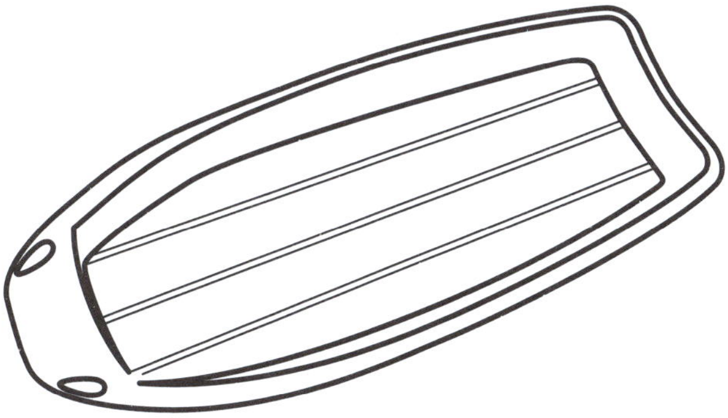

_____ed

_____ug

Got it!　OK　Not yet

You need:

I can write a letter or letters for most consonant and short vowel sounds.

Write the letters **st** to start each word.

______ick

______op

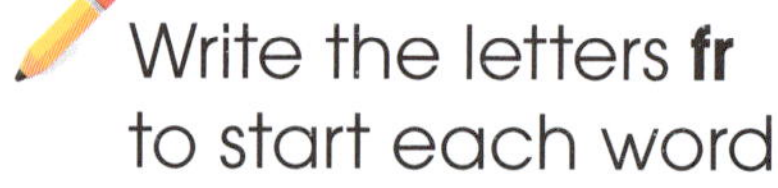

Write the letters **fr** to start each word.

______og

______esh

Got it! OK Not yet

CCSS.ELA-Literacy.L.K.2.C

You need:

I can write a letter or letters for most consonant and short vowel sounds.

Write the letters **tr** to start each word.

Say each word.

Color the pictures.

____ actor

____ uck

____ ash

Got it! OK Not yet

You need:

I can write a letter or letters for most consonant and short vowel sounds.

Circle all of the pictures that start with **dr**.

Got it!

OK

Not yet

CCSS.ELA-Literacy.L.K.2.C

Let's have some fun!

 Color the scene.

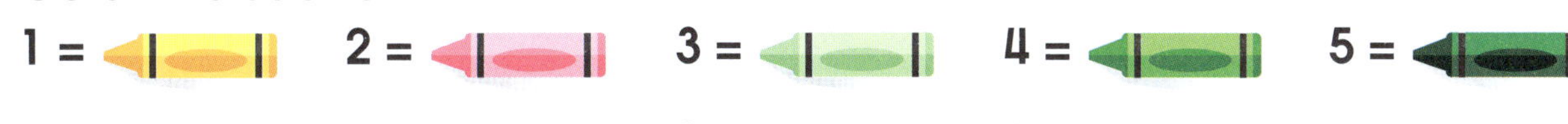

Got it! OK Not yet

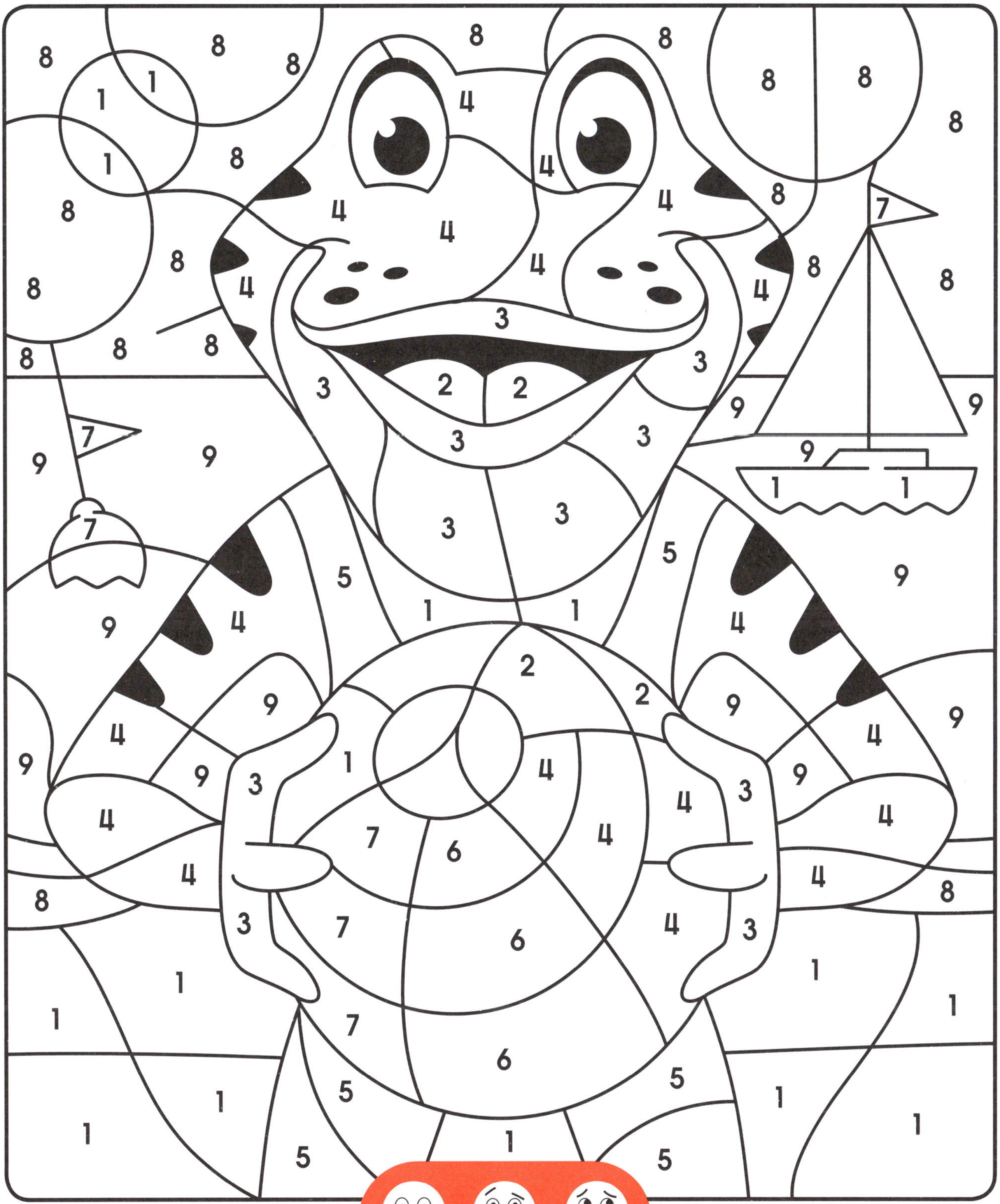

I can correctly name shapes, even when their sizes and positions are different.

Trace the **circles** ◯.
Color the rest of the picture.

Finish drawing the ◯.
Draw a ◯.

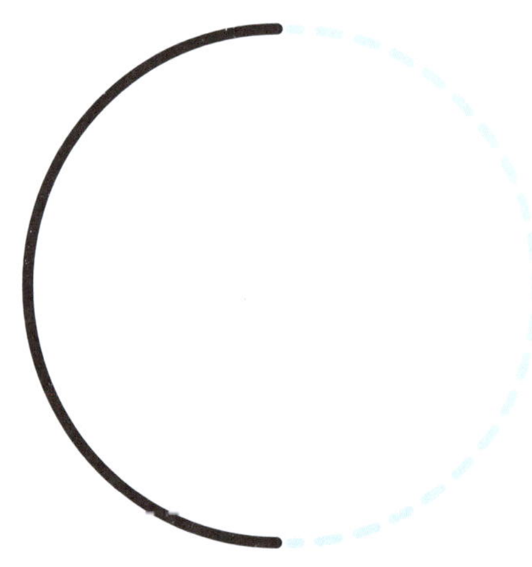

Got it! OK Not yet

CCSS.Math.Content.K.G.B.6

I can correctly name shapes, even when their sizes and positions are different.

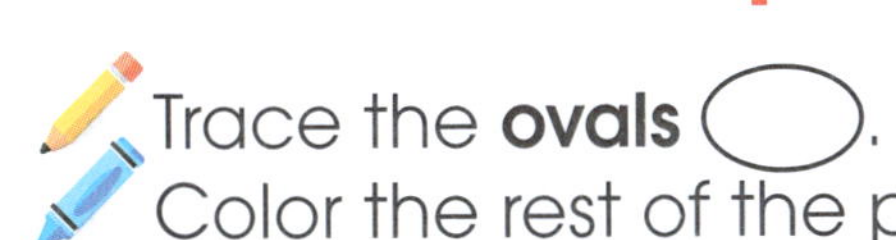

Trace the **ovals** ⬭.
Color the rest of the picture.

Finish drawing the ⬭.
Draw an ⬭.

Got it! OK Not yet

I can use smaller shapes to create one larger shape.

Two **triangles** △▽ can make a **diamond** ◊.
Trace the **triangles** △.
Color the rest of the picture.

Finish drawing the ◊.
Draw a ◊.

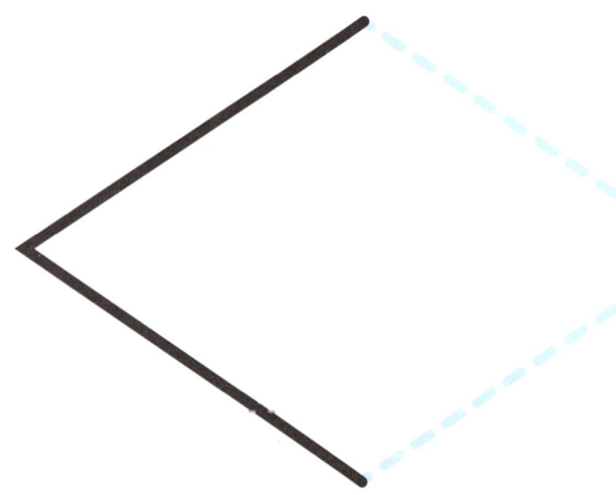

Got it! OK Not yet

CCSS.Math.Content.K.G.B.6

You need:

I can correctly name shapes, even when their sizes and positions are different.

Find things around the house shaped like a **circle**, such as soup cans, a cup or glass, milk bottle caps, coins, etc.

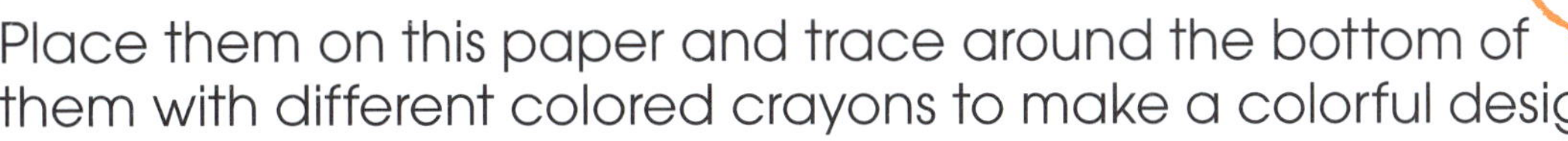

Place them on this paper and trace around the bottom of them with different colored crayons to make a colorful design.

Got it!

OK

Not yet

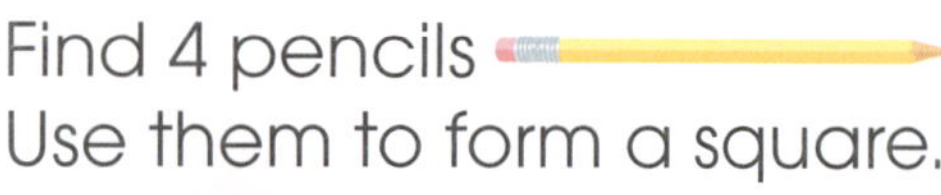

I can make shapes using materials such as clay, sticks, and markers.

You need:

Find 4 pencils.
Use them to form a square.

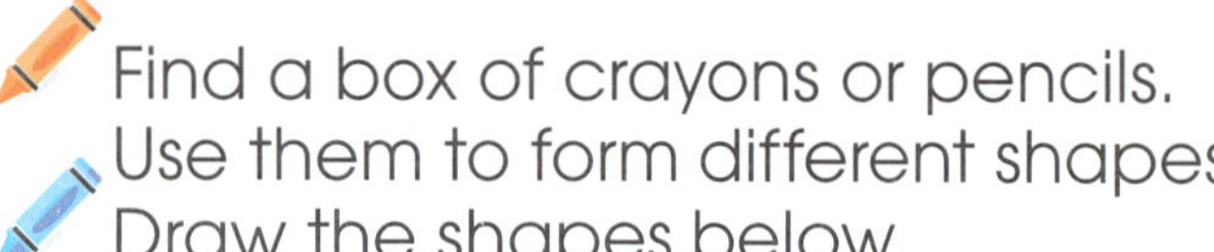

Find a box of crayons or pencils.
Use them to form different shapes.
Draw the shapes below.

Got it! OK Not yet

CCSS.Math.Content.K.G.B.6

You need:

I can make the short and long vowel sounds for each of the five vowels.

Long vowel sounds say the letter name like in the words: **Apes Ate Acorns.** You hear **A** say its name.

Draw a line to each picture that begins with the **long A** sound.

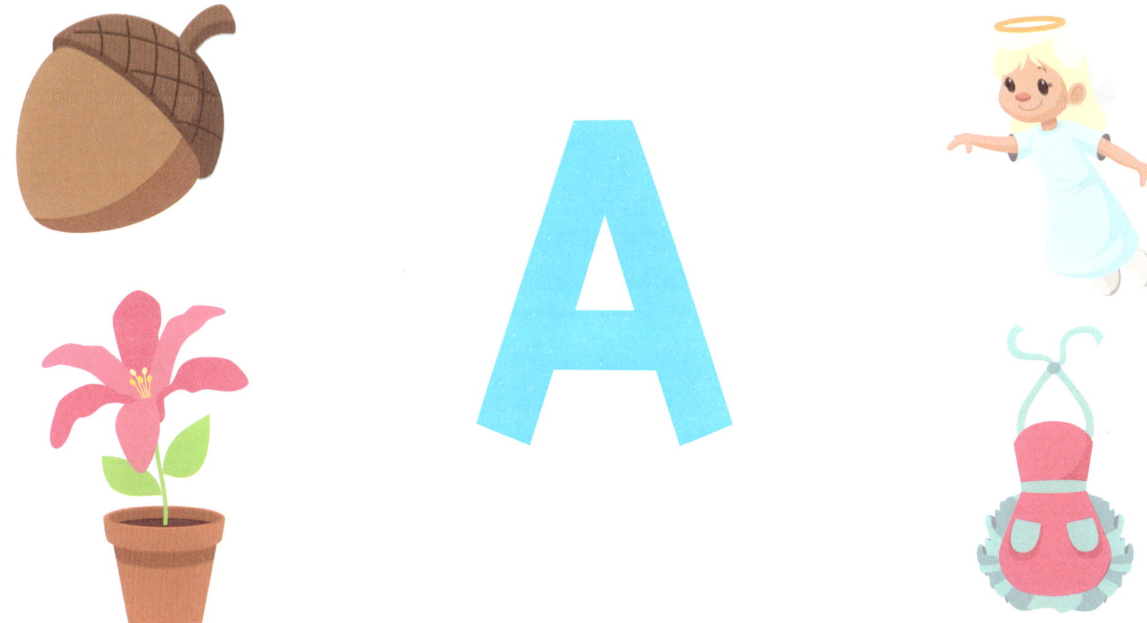

Trace the letters to spell the word.
Start at the red dots (•).

Got it! OK Not yet

I can make the short and long vowel sounds for each of the five vowels.

Draw a line to each picture that begins with the **long E** sound.

Trace the letters to spell the word.
Start at the red dots (•).

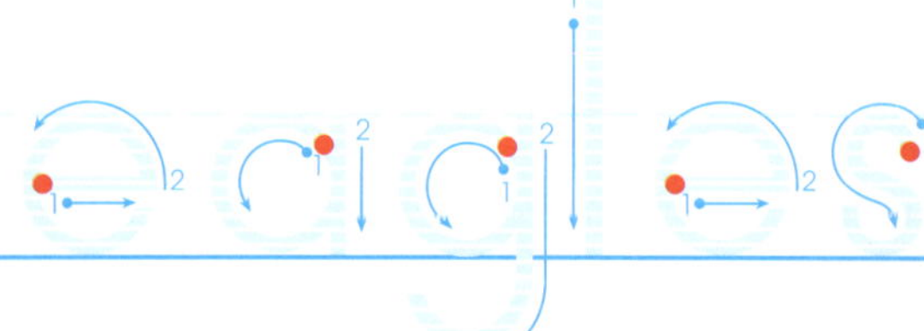

Got it!

OK

Not yet

CCSS.ELA-Literacy.RF.K.3.B

I can make the short and long vowel sounds for each of the five vowels.

You need:

Draw a line to each picture that begins with the **long I** sound.

Trace the letters to spell the word.
Start at the red dots (●).

Got it!

OK

Not yet

I can make the short and long vowel sounds for each of the five vowels.

Ogres Open Oatmeal

Draw a line to each picture that begins with the **long O** sound.

Trace the letters to spell the word.
Start at the red dots (•).

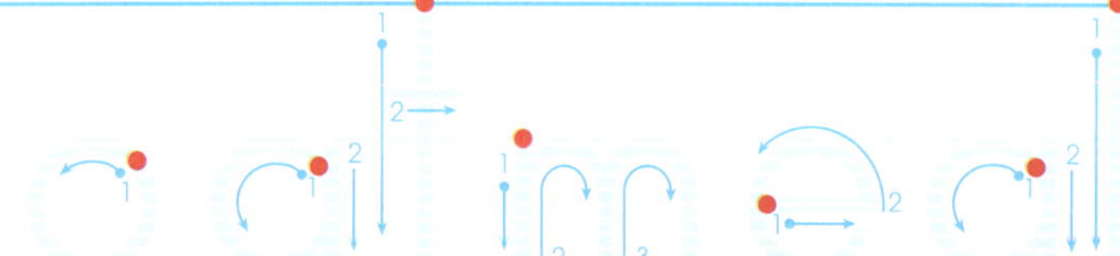

Got it! OK Not yet

CCSS.ELA-Literacy.RF.K.3.B

I can make the short and long vowel sounds for each of the five vowels.

You need:

Unicorns Use Unicycles

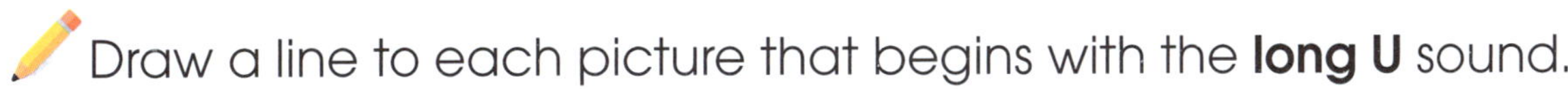

Draw a line to each picture that begins with the **long U** sound.

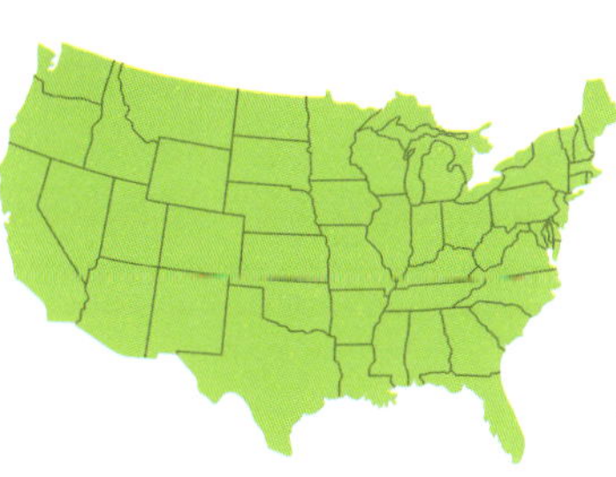

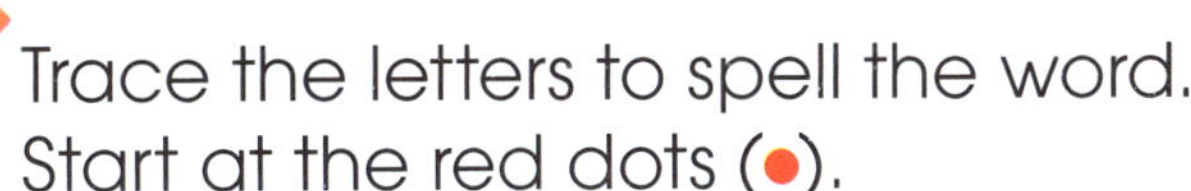

Trace the letters to spell the word.
Start at the red dots (●).

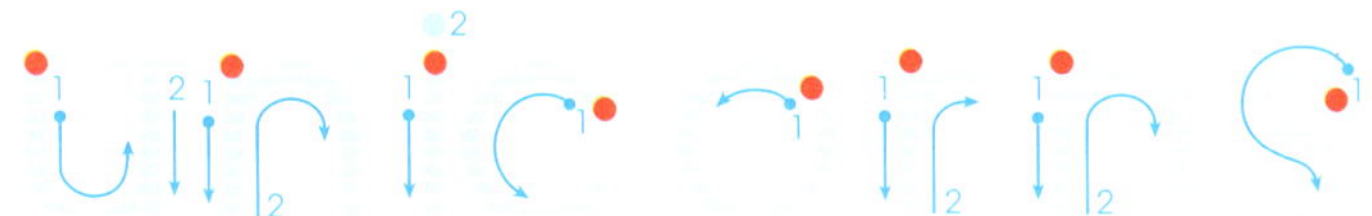

Got it! OK Not yet

I can make the short and long vowel sounds for each of the five vowels.

Say the name of each picture.
Circle the picture that has each **long vowel** sound.

Long a

Long e

Long i

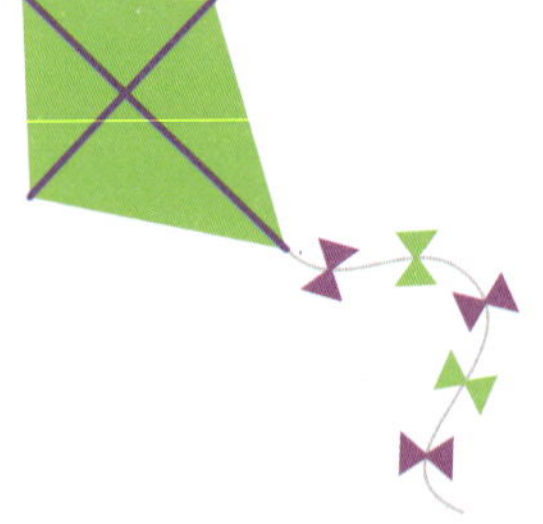

Long o

Long u

Got it!

OK

Not yet

CCSS.ELA-Literacy.RF.K.3.B

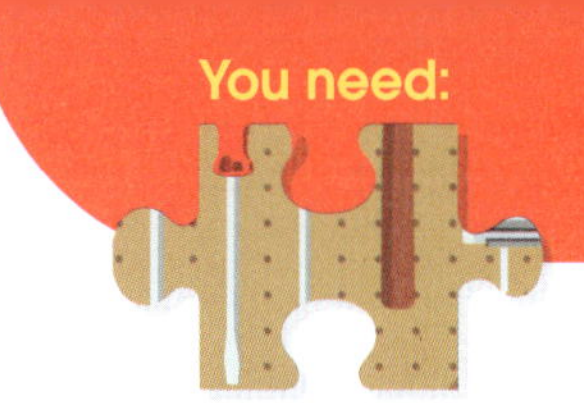

Finish the puzzle.

You need:

Find and place the missing puzzle piece stickers 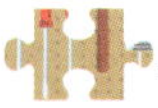.

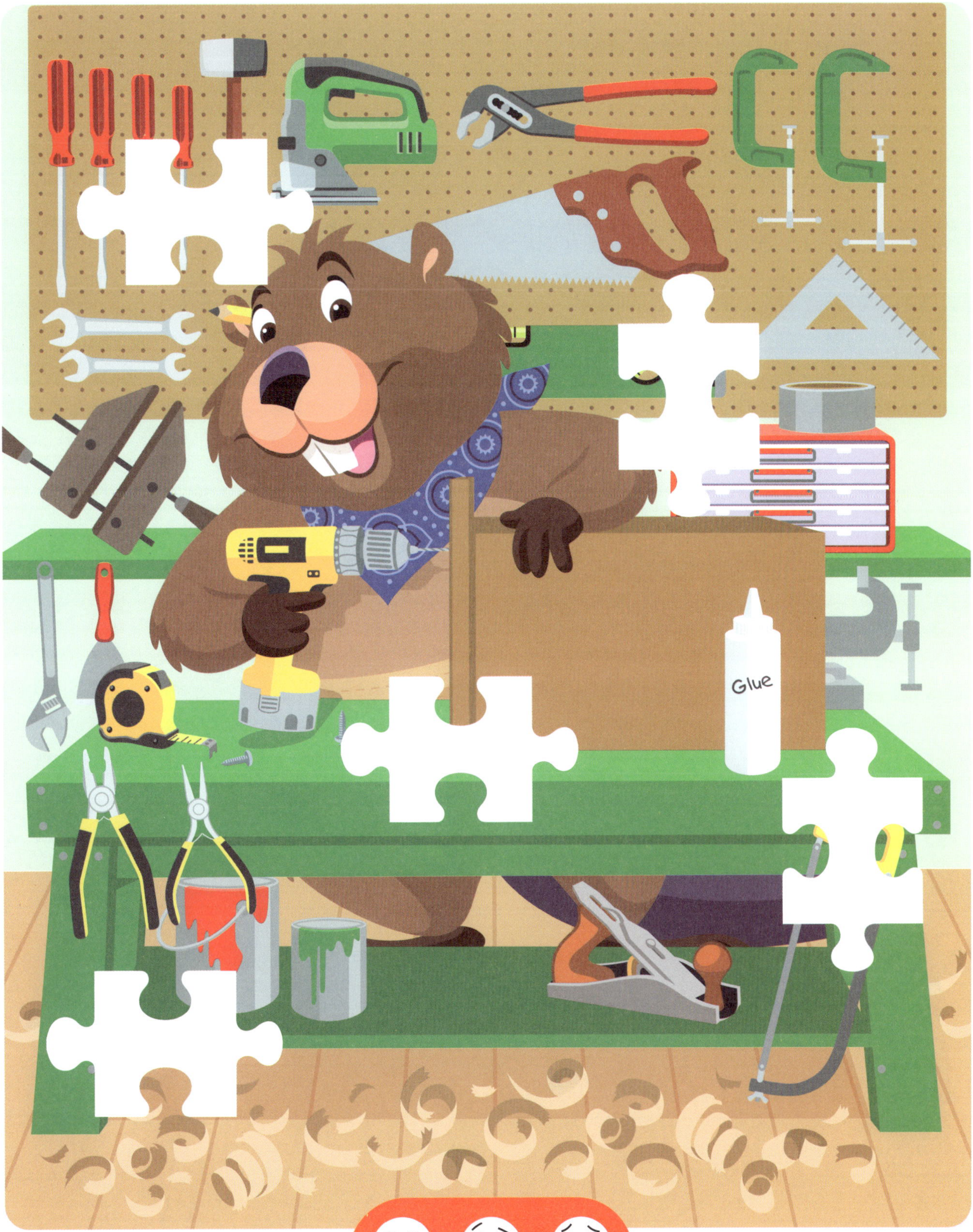

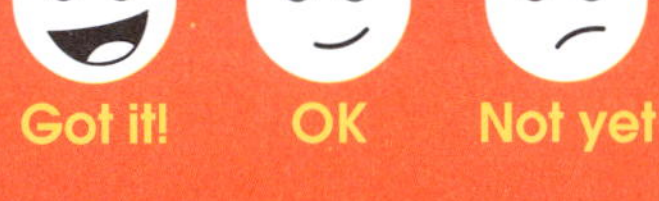

Got it! OK Not yet

Let's have some fun!

 Color the scene.

1 = yellow   2 = pink   3 = green   4 = peach   5 = brown

6 = gray   7 = dark brown   8 = light blue   9 = purple

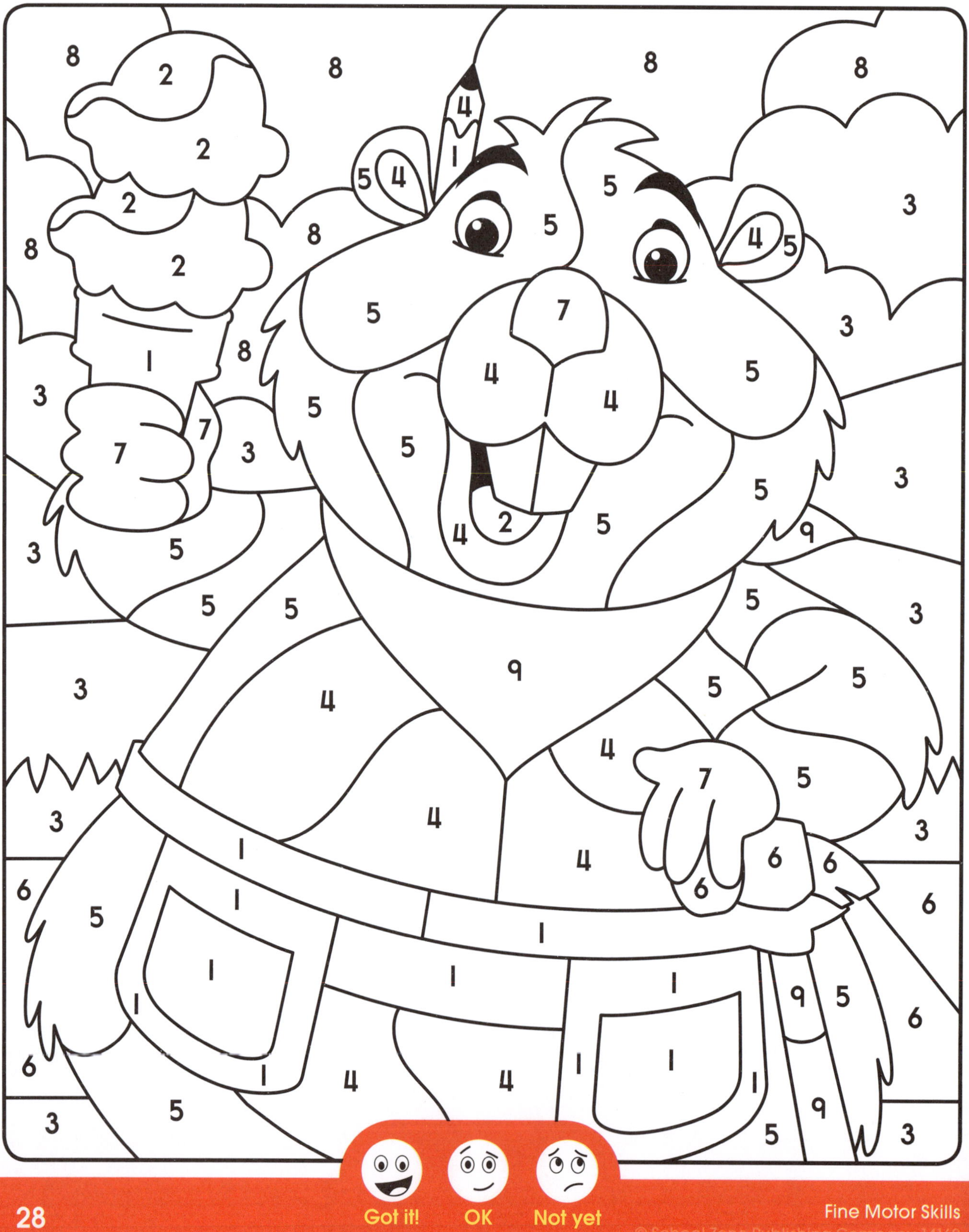

Got it!   OK   Not yet

I can tell if a shape is two-dimensional or three-dimensional.

A **cone** is a shape that looks like this: 

How many [cone] can you find? ____________

Got it! OK Not yet

I can tell if a shape is two-dimensional or three-dimensional.

A **sphere** is a shape that looks like this:

How many [sphere] can you find? ____________

Got it! OK Not yet

CCSS.Math.Content.K.G.A.3

I can tell if a shape is two-dimensional or three-dimensional.

You need:

A **cube** is a shape that looks like this:

How many [cube] can you find? ____________

Got it! OK Not yet

I can tell if a shape is two-dimensional or three-dimensional.

A **cylinder** is a shape that looks like this:

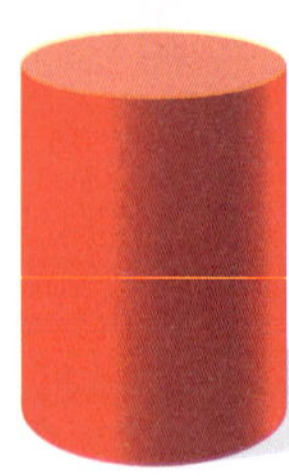

How many [cylinder] can you find? ____________

Got it!   OK   Not yet

CCSS.Math.Content.K.G.A.3

I can make the short and long vowel sounds for each of the five vowels.

Say the name of each picture.
Circle the **long vowel** sound heard in each word.

a e i o u

a e i o u

a e i o u

a e i o u

a e i o u

Got it! OK Not yet

I can add or change sounds in a one-syllable word to make a new word.

You need:

Say **cap**. Then change **c** to **m** and the word is **map**.

Say the name of the first picture in each row.
Circle the letter that you need to change to spell the second picture.

WELCOME

rat → _at

m b

pig → _ig

f w

dog → _og

z l

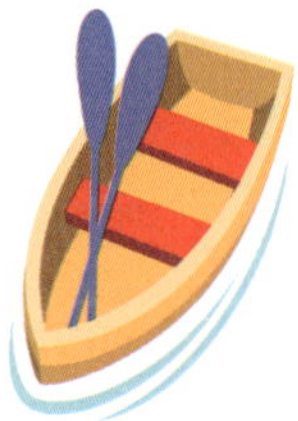

goat → _oat

b p

Got it! OK Not yet

CCSS.ELA-Literacy.RF.K.2.E

I can add or change sounds in a one-syllable word to make a new word.

You need:

Add **ig** to make a new word. Say each word.
Draw a line to the matching picture.

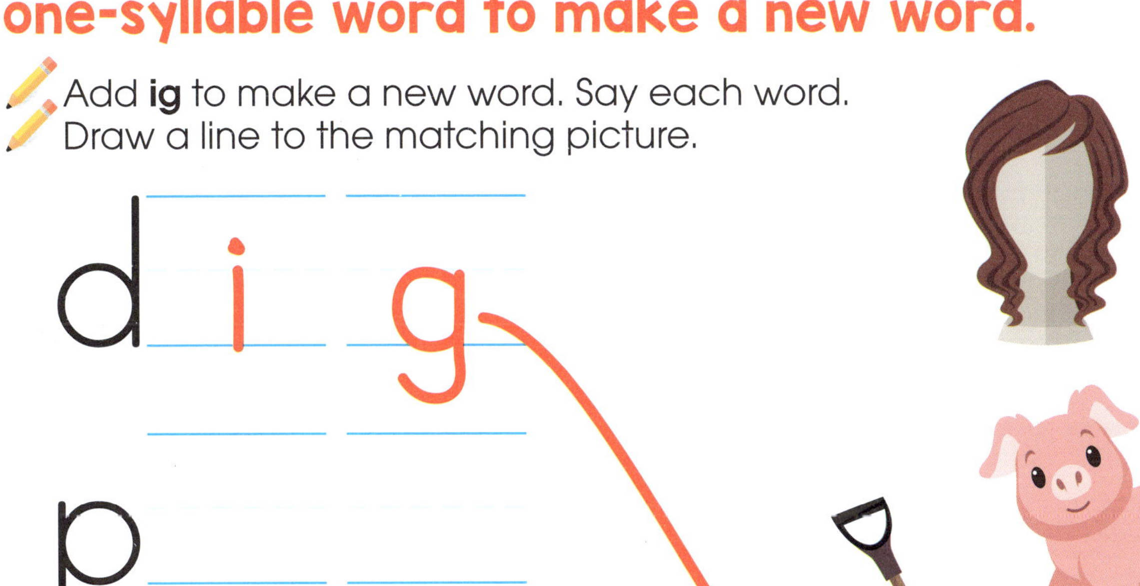

w

Add **og** to make a new word. Say each word.
Draw a line to the matching picture.

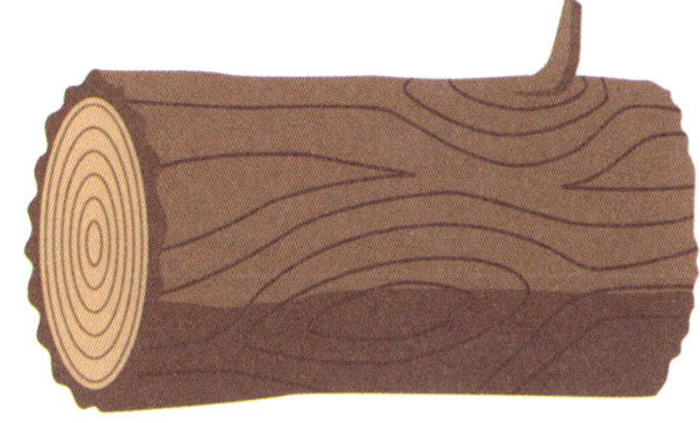

Got it!

OK

Not yet

I can add or change sounds in a one-syllable word to make a new word.

Add **ug** to make a new word. Say each word.
Draw a line to the matching picture.

Add **at** to make a new word. Say each word.
Draw a line to the matching picture.

c

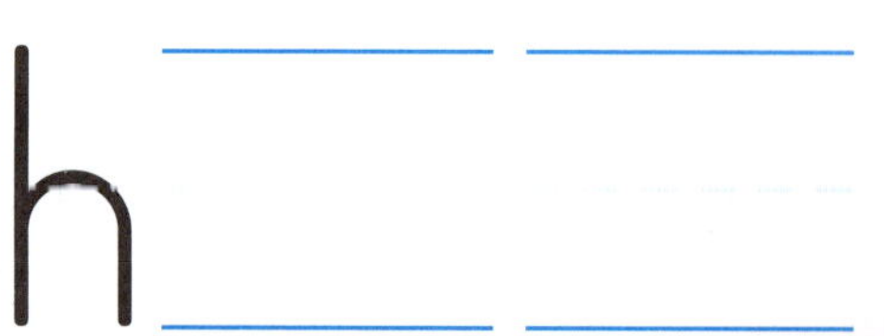

Got it!

OK

Not yet

CCSS.ELA-Literacy.RF.K.2.E

You need:

I can add or change sounds in a one-syllable word to make a new word.

Add **an** to make a new word. Say each word.
Draw a line to the matching picture.

c ___ ___

m ___ ___

v ___ ___

Add **et** to make a new word. Say each word.
Draw a line to the matching picture.

w ___ ___

n ___ ___

j ___ ___

Got it!

OK

Not yet

I can describe the location of objects around me by using words.

You need:

Where is the bird?

on

Color the  **inside** the fence **brown**.

Find and place the  stickers **outside** the fence.

Find and place the  stickers **on** the fence.

Let's have some fun!

You need:

Help the flamingo get to its friend.
Draw a line through the maze from **start** to **finish**.

Got it! OK Not yet

I can describe the location of objects around me by using words.

in

under

over

What is **over** the bookcase?

What is **under** the bookcase?

What is **in** the bookcase?

Got it! OK Not yet

CCSS.Math.Content.K.G.A.1

I can use common prepositions.

You need: ✏️

over under

inside by

Circle the correct word to finish each sentence.

The bird is ________ the doghouse. **over under inside by**

The cat is ________ the doghouse. **over under inside by**

The mouse is ________ the doghouse. **over under inside by**

The dog is ________ the doghouse. **over under inside by**

Got it! OK Not yet

I can describe the location of objects around me by using words.

left

right

Circle the people who are going **left**.
Check the cars that are going **right**.

Got it! OK Not yet

CCSS.Math.Content.K.G.A.1

I can use common prepositions.

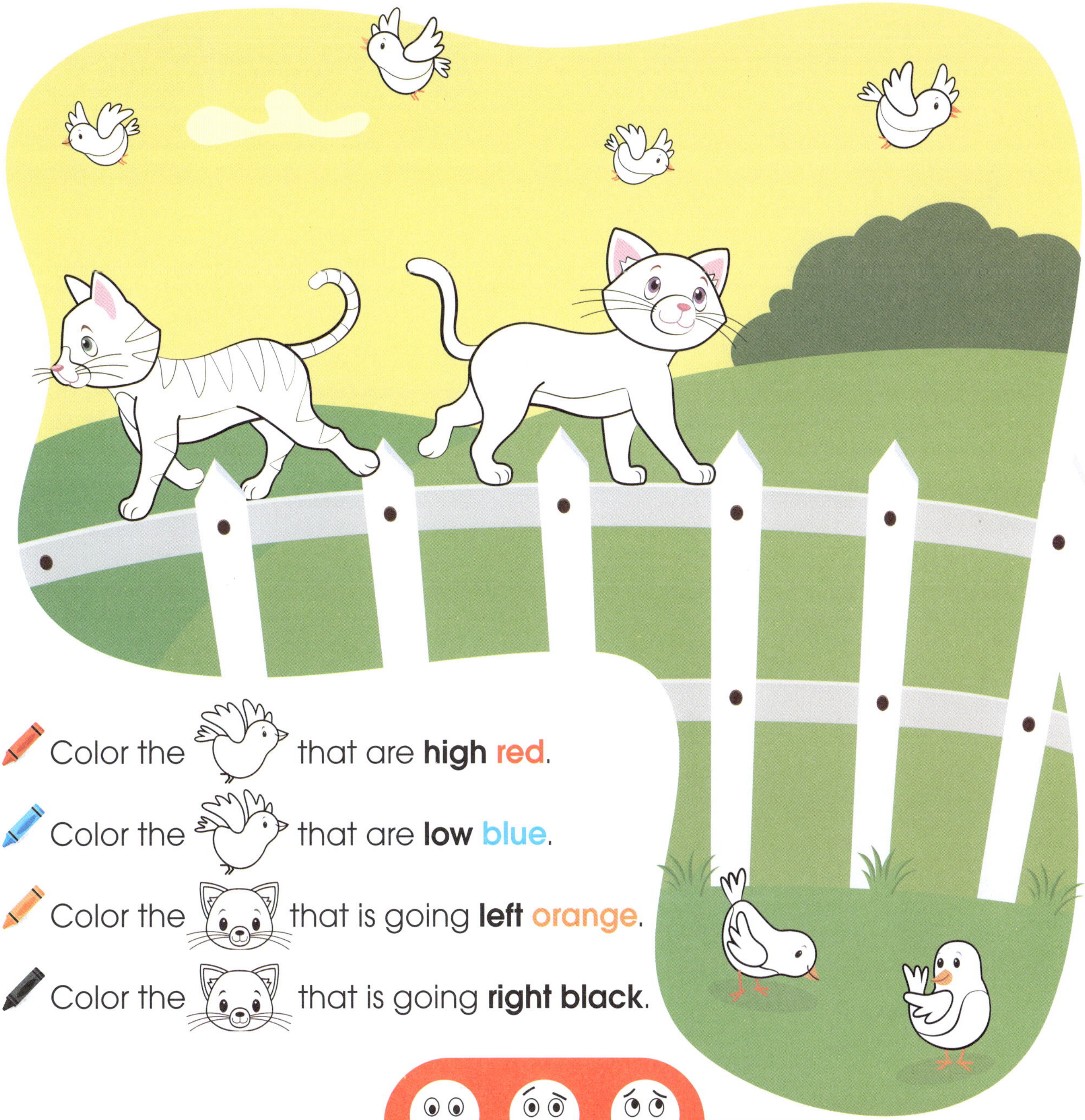

Color the [bird] that are **high** red.

Color the [bird] that are **low** blue.

Color the [cat] that is going **left** orange.

Color the [cat] that is going **right black**.

Got it! OK Not yet

I can describe the location of objects around me by using words.

 Draw lines to match the **opposites**.

left

low

high

inside

outside

right

Got it!

OK

Not yet

I can describe objects around me by using shape names.

Color the objects that have the same shape as the first one.

Got it! OK Not yet

You need:

I can describe objects around me by using shape names.

Draw lines from the objects to the matching shapes.

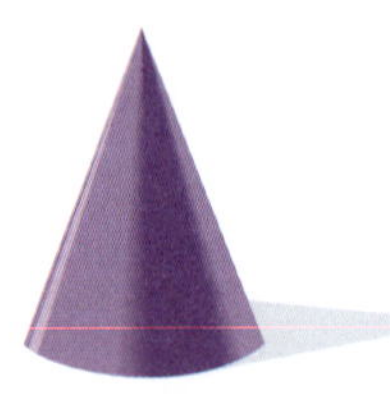

Got it! OK Not yet

CCSS.Math.Content.K.G.A.3

I can spell words by listening to the sounds that I hear.

You need:

Say the name of each picture out loud. Spell the words.

Got it! OK Not yet

I can spell words by listening to the sounds that I hear.

Say the name of each picture out loud.
Spell the words.

You need:

Got it!

OK

Not yet

CCSS.ELA-Literacy.L.K.2.D

I can use common nouns and verbs.

You need:

Nouns are people, places, and things.

people
me, mom, us

places
park, house, playground

things
bus, bike, sign

Find and place the noun stickers  in the correct noun boxes.

people	places	things

Got it! OK Not yet

You need:

I can use common nouns and verbs.

Nouns can be people.

Help the family get home.

Draw a line connecting all of the words that name **people**.

Got it! OK Not yet

CCSS.ELA-Literacy.L.K.1.B

I can use common nouns and verbs.

You need:

Nouns can be places.

Read the riddles.

Write the answers on the lines.

This is where you learn.

This is where you buy things.

This is where a family can live.

This is where many people live and work.

This is where you play in the sand.

Got it! OK Not yet

I can use common nouns and verbs.

You need:

eggs
juice
bread
ham
apple
milk

Nouns can be things.

Write the words that fit the shapes.

e

a

b

m

h

j

Which food rhymes with **legs**?

CCSS.ELA-Literacy.L.K.1.B

You need:

I can read common words.

Find and circle the words in the list below.
Words are only going across.

GO	HERE	MAKE	FIND
AWAY	HELP	PLAY	FUNNY

J	M	L	A	W	A	Y	G	O	I
A	S	A	Z	S	N	A	T	D	O
F	I	N	D	I	H	E	R	E	O
R	O	C	H	P	U	Q	P	N	Y
M	P	L	A	Y	S	R	U	K	H
R	F	U	N	N	Y	Y	G	C	M
K	I	X	J	D	V	P	L	D	F
X	F	N	U	J	T	M	A	K	E
Q	A	H	E	L	P	U	D	D	O
W	K	K	Q	H	B	F	A	E	N

Got it! OK Not yet

I can read common words.

You need:

Read the poem.

Circle the word **my**.

Underline the word **go**.

I told my dog to go away.
Where did he go?
I want to play.
Look down here.
That is funny!
Is that my dog or a
big brown bunny?

Parent Tip:
Have your child read the poem with silly voices. Have them try talking like a robot, a cowboy/cowgirl, or underwater.

Got it!

OK

Not yet

CCSS.ELA-Literacy.RF.K.3.C

You need:

I can read common words.

Draw a line from each word to the matching picture. The first one is done for you.

run

two

jump

three

Got it!

OK

Not yet

I can use common nouns and verbs.

You need:

A **verb** is an action word.

Draw lines to match the **action words**.

run

hop

swing

sit

hop

run

sit

swing

Got it!

OK

Not yet

CCSS.ELA-Literacy.L.K.1.B

You need:

I can use common nouns and verbs.

A **verb** is an action word.

Circle the action words in the puzzle.

Words are only going across and down.

kick	play	dig	laugh
climb	jump	hop	push

j	u	m	p	b	p	y	n
k	n	o	x	l	u	q	k
c	x	r	y	j	s	v	i
l	u	d	i	g	h	z	c
i	l	a	u	g	h	y	k
m	g	d	z	h	o	p	a
b	a	p	c	p	l	a	y

Got it!

OK

Not yet

You need:

I can show that I understand common verbs by talking about their opposites.

Draw a line from the picture to the word that describes the picture. The first one is done for you.

running

walking

The girl is ______.

The girl is ______.

eating

drinking

The dog is ______.

The dog is ______.

waking up

sleeping

The boy is ______.

The boy is ______.

Got it!

OK

Not yet

CCSS.ELA-Literacy.L.K.5.B

I can show that I understand common verbs by talking about their opposites.

 Draw a line from the picture to the word that describes the picture.

The boy is ______.

laughing

crying

The boy is ______.

The squirrel is ______.

whispering

shouting

The squirrel is ______.

The girl is ______.

sitting

standing

The girl is ______.

Got it!

OK

Not yet

I can show someone how I add or subtract by drawing pictures, using objects, using my fingers, or any other method.

How many **are left**?
Write the number.
The first one is done for you.

3 − 2 = 1

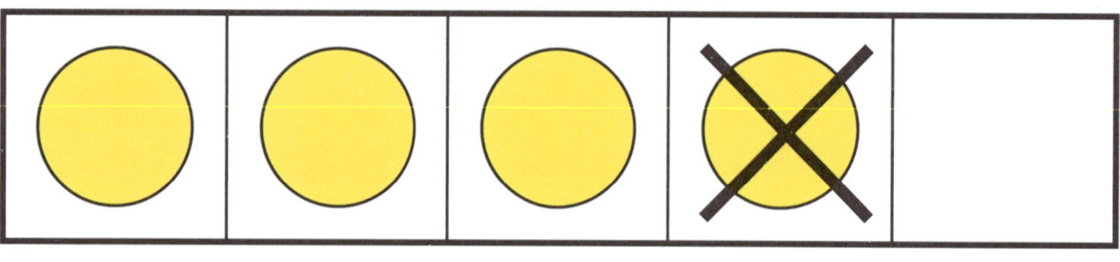

4 − 1 = ____

5 − 3 = ____

Got it! OK Not yet

CCSS.Math.Content.K.OA.A.1

I can show someone how I add or subtract by drawing pictures, using objects, using my fingers, or any other method.

How many **are left**?
Write the number.

5 – 4 = ____

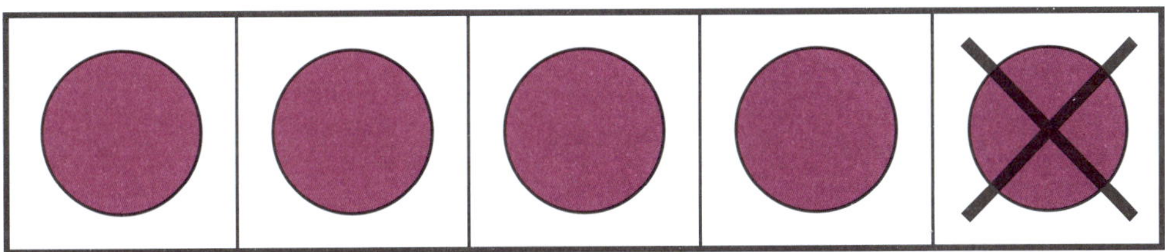

5 – 1 = ____

4 – 2 = ____

Got it! OK Not yet

I can show someone how I add or subtract by drawing pictures, using objects, using my fingers, or any other method.

How many **are left**?
Write the number.

2 - 1 = ____

4 - 2 = ____

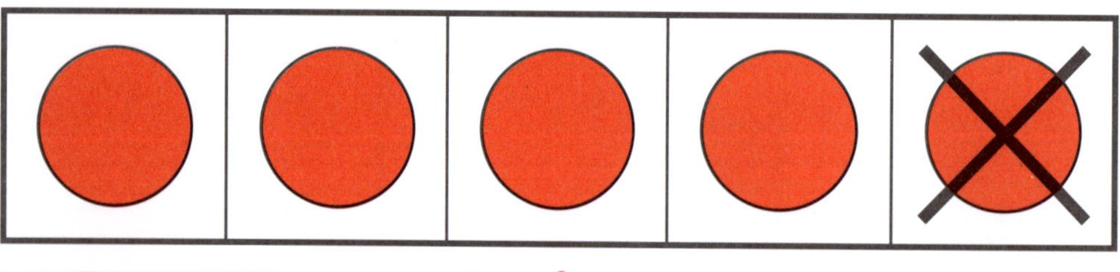

5 - 1 = ____

Got it! OK Not yet

CCSS.Math.Content.K.OA.A.1

I can show someone how I add or subtract by drawing pictures, using objects, using my fingers, or any other method.

How many **are left**?
Write the missing numbers.

___ – ___ = ___

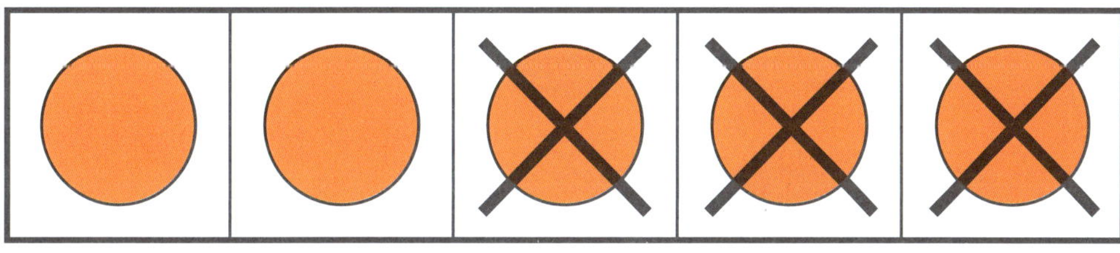

___ – ___ = ___

___ – ___ = ___

Got it! OK Not yet

You need:

Let's have some fun!

 Color the scene.

1 = 2 = 3 =

4 = 5 = 6 =

Got it! OK Not yet

I can capitalize the first word in a sentence and the pronoun I.

Cut out the booklet below and fold along the center line.
Write the letter **M** to finish each sentence.

My dog!

Fold along this line.

My dog!

______y dog
is yellow.

______y dog
is Charlie!

I can capitalize the first word in a sentence and the pronoun I.

Cut out the booklet below and fold along the center line.
Write the letter **M** to start each sentence.
Place these pages inside the pages from page 65.
Read the book out loud.

___y dog
likes to run.

Fold along this line.

___y dog
is fast.

______y dog
likes to eat.

______y dog
is fun.

You need:

I can explain how the pictures and words in a story work together in a story with help.

Underline the sentence that goes with the picture. The first one is done for you.

I see a ball.

I see a dog.

I see a bird.

I see a cat.

I see a car.

I see a bike.

I see a bat.

I see ball.

Got it!

OK

Not yet

I can explain how the pictures and words in a story work together in a story with help.

Underline the sentence that goes with the picture.

There is one.

There are two.

It is green.

It is red.

It is big.

It is little.

It is tall.

It is short.

CCSS.ELA-Literacy.RL.K.7

I can write, draw, and tell someone what topic I am reading about and then tell them about what I know about that topic.

Informational writing teaches us about something. One type can teach us how to do something.

Abe wrote about how to make a sandwich.

First, I get the bread.

Then, I add the peanut butter and jelly.

Last, I eat it. Yum!

Got it! OK Not yet

I can write and add to complete sentences with an adult and/or other kindergarteners.

You need:

Informational writing teaches using a lot of details.

Mya wrote about how to build a snowman.

First, you make a ball for the body.

Then, you make a ball for the head.

Write what is on the snowman, but missing in the sentence.

Last, you add a hat, a carrot nose, a scarf, and

________________________.

Got it! OK Not yet

CCSS.ELA-Literacy.L.K.1.F

You need:

I can write and add to complete sentences with an adult and/or other kindergarteners.

How to Set a Table

First, put the plate on the table.

Then, add a napkin and a cup.

Next, add a knife and a fork.

Write what is missing on the table.

Last, add a ______________________

______________________.

Got it! OK Not yet

You need:

I can write and add to complete sentences with an adult and/or other kindergarteners.

Sarah wrote about how to pack a backpack.

First, put in a book.

Then, put in a notebook.

Next, put in your lunch.

Write what is in the backpack, but missing in the sentence.

Last, you need a snack, so you put in a ______________

______________.

Got it!

OK

Not yet

CCSS.ELA-Literacy.L.K.1.F

You need:

I can write, draw, and tell someone what topic I am reading about and then tell them about what I know about that topic.

Informational writing can give us information in the pictures.

Carter wrote about how to draw a house.
Help Carter add to his pictures to give information.

First, draw a square □ for the house.

Then, draw a triangle △ for the roof.

Last, draw a door and windows ⊞.

Got it! OK Not yet

You need:

I can write, draw, and tell someone what topic I am reading about and then tell them about what I know about that topic.

Read the instructions on how to rake leaves. Draw a picture of each step.

First, you rake the leaves into a big pile.

Then, you run and jump.

Last, you toss leaves in the air.

Got it!

OK

Not yet

I can write, draw, and tell someone what topic I am reading about and then tell them about what I know about that topic.

Write an **informational writing** about something you know how to do.
Draw pictures to help tell your story.
Draw your pictures first to help plan what you are going to write.

First,

Then,

Got it!

OK

Not yet

Parent Tip:
Make your child feel like an author, and help them share their writing with relatives through technology.

You need:

Last,

Writing Checklist:

- [ ] I told my steps in order.
- [ ] I used a capital letter at the beginning of each sentence.
- [ ] I added pictures.
- [ ] I used a (.) or (!) at the end of each sentence.

Got it!

OK

Not yet

CCSS.ELA-Literacy.W.K.2

You need:

I can show someone how I add or subtract by drawing pictures, using objects, using my fingers, or any other method.

How many **are left**?
Write the number.

5 - 1 = ______

3 - 2 = ______

3 - 3 = ______

4 - 2 = ______

Got it! OK Not yet

You need:

I can show someone how I add or subtract by drawing pictures, using objects, using my fingers, or any other method.

How many **are left**?
Write the number.

7 – 2 = ______

6 – 3 = ______

9 – 3 = ______

8 – 4 = ______

Got it! OK Not yet

CCSS.Math.Content.K.OA.A.1

I can show someone how I add or subtract by drawing pictures, using objects, using my fingers, or any other method.

How many **are left**?
Write the number.

______

$9 - 5 =$ ______

______

$7 - 6 =$ ______

______

$10 - 3 =$ ______

______

$4 - 3 =$ ______

Got it! OK Not yet

You need:

I can show someone how I add or subtract by drawing pictures, using objects, using my fingers, or any other method.

How many **are left**?
Write the number.

8 - 1 = ______

5 - 3 = ______

10 - 6 = ______

6 - 1 = ______

Got it! OK Not yet

CCSS.Math.Content.K.OA.A.1

You need:

I can show someone how I add or subtract by drawing pictures, using objects, using my fingers, or any other method.

How many **are left**?
Circle the group that matches the number.

6 – 2 =

8 – 6 =

7 – 1 =

9 – 3 =

Got it! OK Not yet

You need:

I can use objects or drawings to solve subtraction word problems up to 10.

Read the word problems.
Write the subtraction number sentences.

Addison had **8** ice pops.
She gave **4 away**.
How many does she **have left**?

____ − ____ = ____

Luke has **10** toy cars in front of him.
He pushes **5** of them away.
How many **are left** in front of him?

____ − ____ = ____

Got it! OK Not yet

CCSS.Math.Content.K.OA.A.2

I can subtract numbers within 5.

You need:

Write your answers.

5 - 3 = ____

2 - 2 = ____

3 - 1 = ____

4 - 1 = ____

2 - 2 = ____

5 - 0 = ____

5 - 1 = ____

3 - 2 = ____

4 - 2 = ____

4 - 4 = ____

2 - 1 = ____

GOAL!
Try to get 10 correct in **1 minute**.

You need:

I can subtract numbers within 5.

Write your answers.

$4 - 3 =$ ____

$5 - 4 =$ ____

$3 - 2 =$ ____

$3 - 1 =$ ____

$5 - 5 =$ ____

$5 - 1 =$ ____

$4 - 0 =$ ____

$2 - 2 =$ ____

$5 - 2 =$ ____

$4 - 2 =$ ____

$4 - 1 =$ ____

$5 - 3 =$ ____

Got it!

OK

Not yet

CCSS.Math.Content.K.OA.A.5

Let's have some fun!

Draw a line through the maze to help the baby sheep find his family.

start

finish

Got it! OK Not yet

Let's have some fun!

You need:

Draw a line through the maze to help the monkey find his bananas.

Got it! OK Not yet

You need:

I can read and understand kindergarten books.

Parents:
Please read the book **Underwater** to your child.
Then ask the following questions.

Why did the author write this book?

To teach us how to swim.

To teach us about fish.

What word describes a picture of this fish?

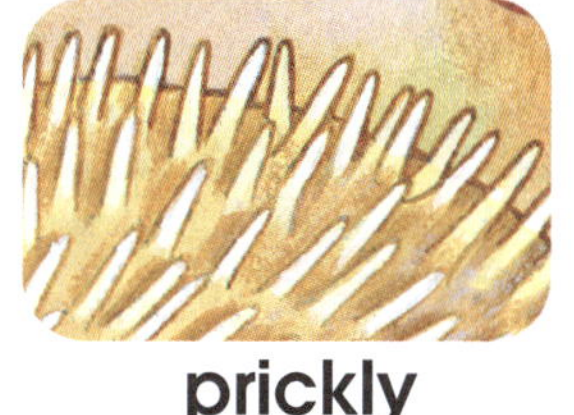

prickly

striped

Look at this picture.

What words go with this picture?

Some fish have a light.

Some fish like to bite.

What word best describes this fish's face?

frown

smile

What color is the fish that is swimming upside down?

purple **blue**

Got it!

OK

Not yet

CCSS.ELA-Literacy.RF.K.4

I can figure out the connections between words with an adult's help.

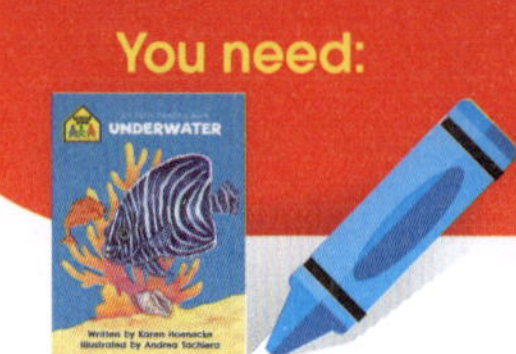

 Read the **Underwater** book.

 Color the **scales** blue.

 Color the **coral** pink.

Parent Tip:
To best help your child with vocabulary, read to your child and stop and talk about unknown words.

Got it! OK Not yet

CCSS.ELA-Literacy.L.K.5

I can take apart a number from 11-19 by splitting it into tens and the leftover ones.

Each ● = 1, each [ten-frame] = 10.

13 = 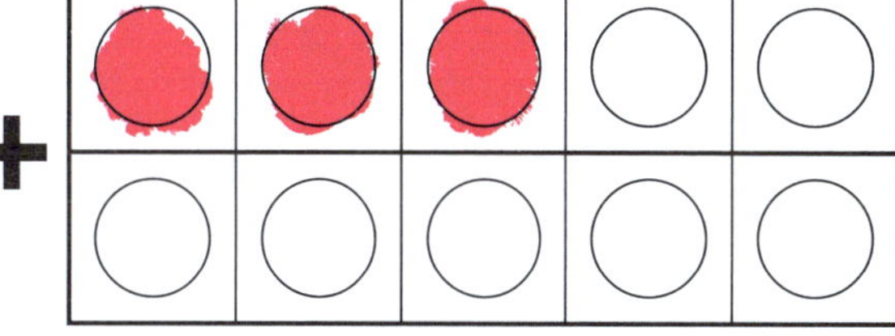

Read the number in each row.
Color the dots to match the number.

15 = 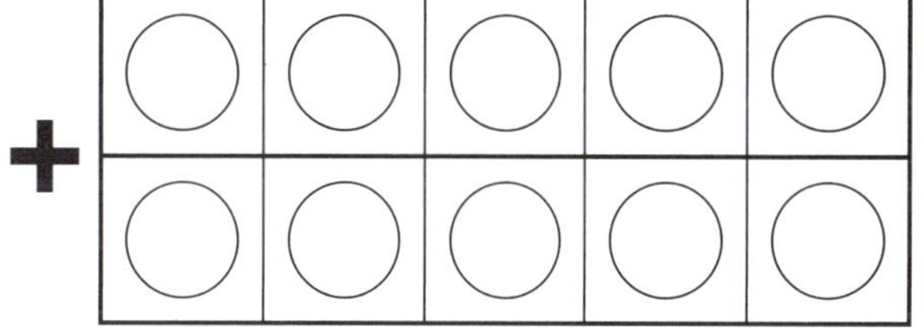

14 = 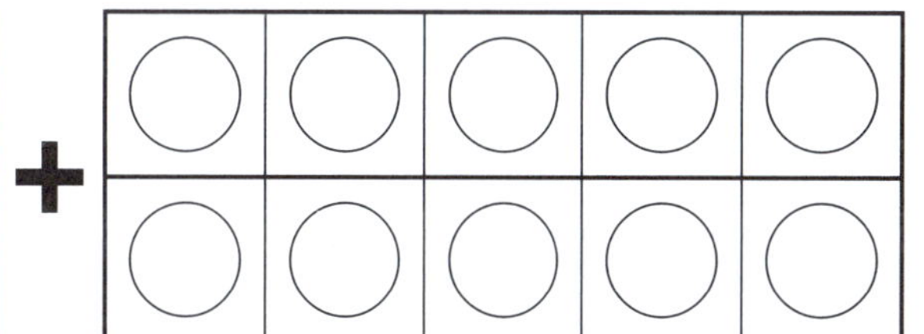

17 = 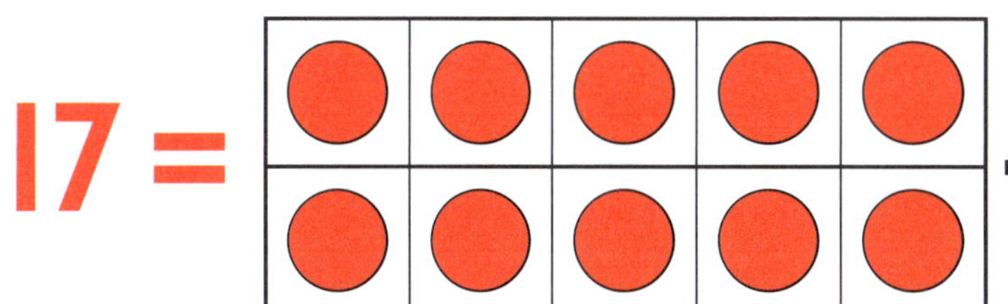 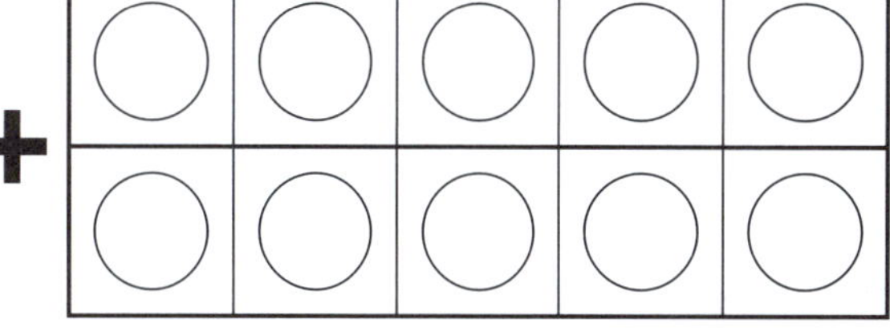

19 = 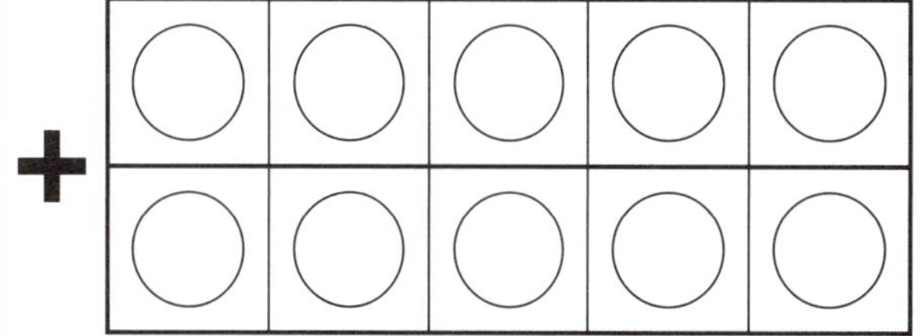

Got it! OK Not yet

I can make a number from 11-19 and show that it is made up of a group of ten and some ones.

You need:

How many buttons are there?

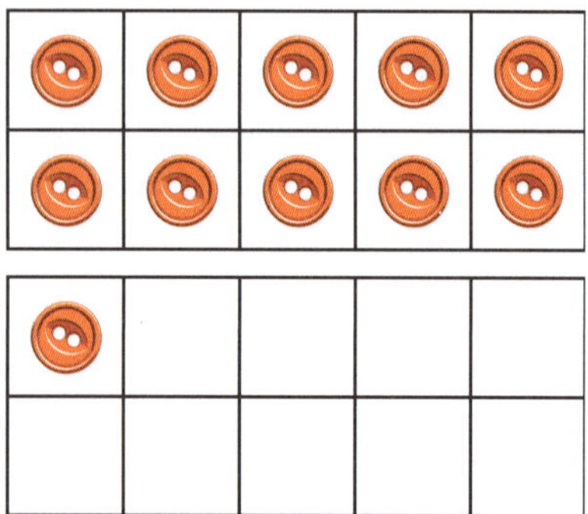

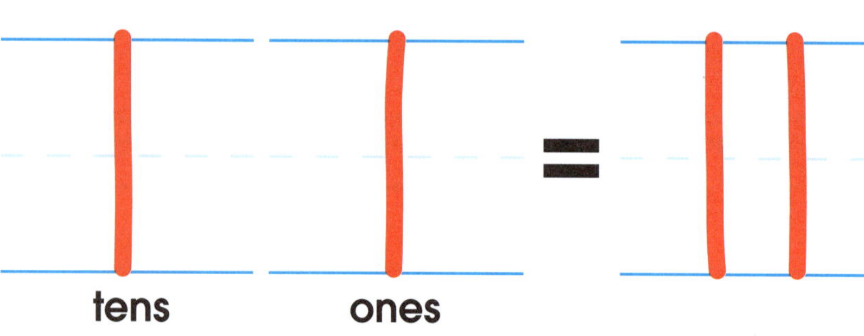

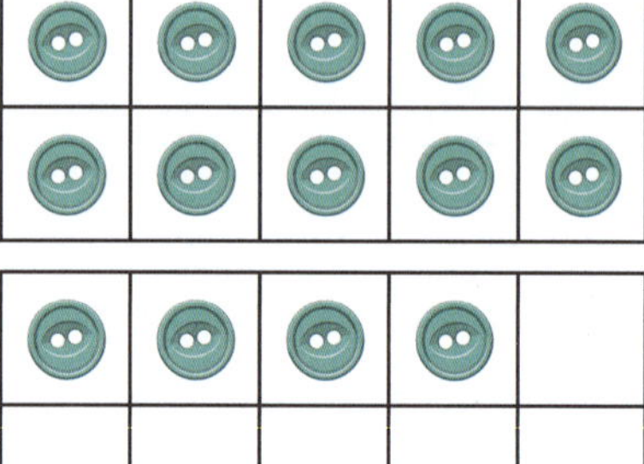

___ tens ___ ones = ___

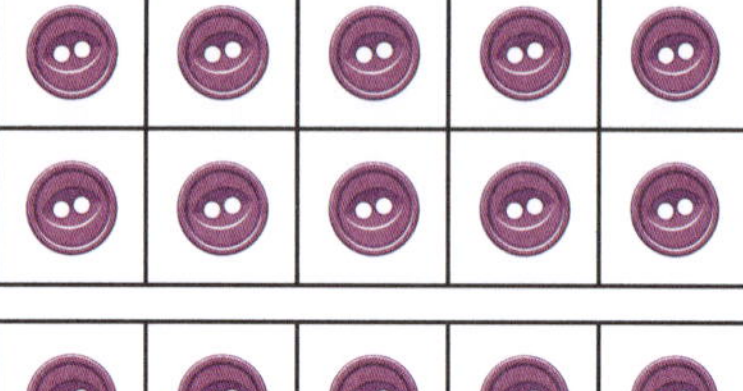

___ tens ___ ones = ___

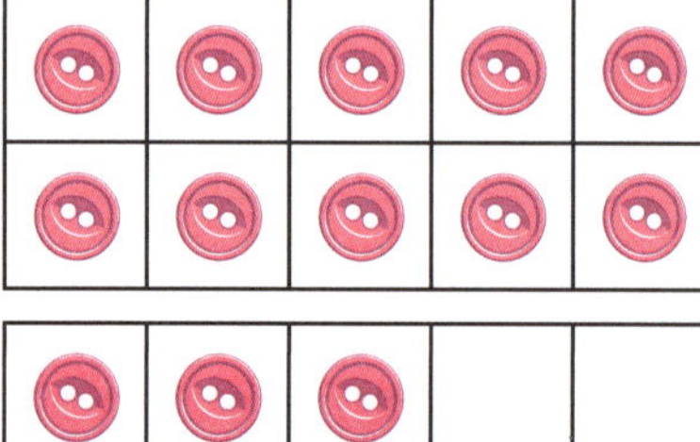

___ tens ___ ones = ___

Got it!

OK

Not yet

CCSS.Math.Content.K.NBT.A.1

I can make a number from 11-19 and show that it is made up of a group of ten and some ones.

You need:

Write how many pieces of fruit there are in each group.

_____ _____ = _____

tens ones

_____ _____ = _____

tens ones

_____ _____ = _____

tens ones

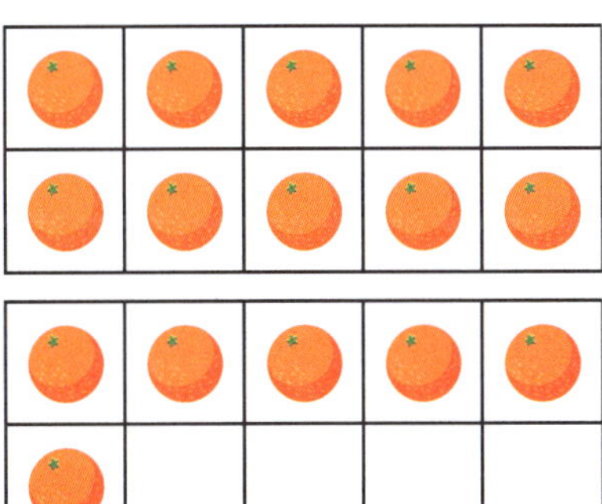

_____ _____ = _____

tens ones

Got it!

OK

Not yet

You need:

I can figure out the connections between words with an adult's help.

Find and place the stickers to finish the sentences.

I looked out the window.

I saw it was raining.

I put 

on my feet.

I put on my 

. I used the 

to stay dry.

CCSS.ELA-Literacy.L.K.5

Two of a Kind

You need:

Look at each of the pictures.

Circle the two pictures that are the same.

Got it! OK Not yet

I can figure out the connections between words with an adult's help.

Where is the fish?

over

under

inside

by

Circle the correct word to finish each sentence.

The [seagull] is ______ the boat. over under inside by

The [fish] are ______ the boat. over under inside by

The [turtle] is ______ the boat. over under inside by

The [dog] is ______ the boat. over under inside by

Got it!

OK

Not yet

CCSS.ELA-Literacy.L.K.4.A

You need:

I can figure out the connections between words with an adult's help.

high

low

left

right

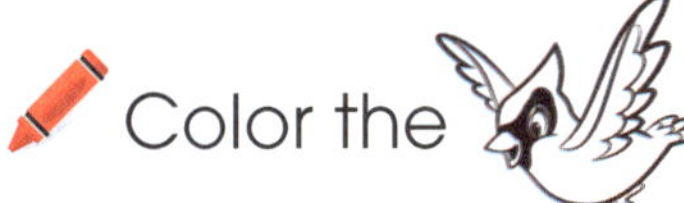

Color the  that are **high** red.

Color the   that are **low** blue.

Color the that is going **right** orange.

Color the that is going **left** gray.

Got it!

OK

Not yet

I can figure out the connections between words with an adult's help.

You need:

Draw a line to match the **action words**.
The first one is done for you.

slide

climb

climb

jump

dig

slide

jump

dig

Got it!

OK

Not yet

CCSS.ELA-Literacy.L.K.5

I can figure out the connections between words with an adult's help.

 Draw a line to match the **opposite words**.

clean

dry

wet

awake

up

dirty

sleeping

down

Got it!

OK

Not yet

You need:

I can write an answer to a question by using what I know and learning more with an adult's help.

A zoo has many helpers to take care of the animals.
Read the clues.
Write the names under the correct pictures.

Bob keeps the animals' homes clean.
Tom helps sick animals.
Deb works with sea animals.
Sam feeds the bears.

Got it! OK Not yet

CCSS.ELA-Literacy.W.K.8

I can write an answer to a question by using what I know and learning more with an adult's help.

✓ Read the clues and put a check mark on the chart for each clue. The first one is done for you.

1. We had fruit.
2. Dad and Tim had tacos.
3. Mom had a salad.
4. Kim had a turkey sandwich.
5. Mom, Tim, and Kim had juice.
6. Dad had milk.

	milk	juice	fruit	salad	taco	sandwich
Dad			✓			
Mom			✓			
Tim			✓			
Kim			✓			

Write the names under the correct meals.

Got it! OK Not yet

I can show how similar verbs are different by acting them out.

All of these words are a way of moving forward.

Write the word to finish each sentence.

I can ______________________ like a monster.

I can ______________________ like a snake.

I can ______________________ like a horse.

I can ______________________ like a kangaroo.

I can ______________________ like a penguin.

CCSS.ELA-Literacy.L.K.5.D

You need:

I can show how similar verbs are different by acting them out.

All of these words are a way of moving up.

float

jump

climb

fly

Write the word to finish each sentence.

I can ______________________ like a monkey.

I can ______________________ like a frog.

I can ______________________ like a bird.

I can ________________ like a jellyfish.

Got it! OK Not yet

I can use common nouns and verbs.

You need:

run

Find and place the **action word** sticker  by the matching action.

place sticker here

place sticker here

place sticker here

place sticker here

place sticker here

Got it! OK Not yet

CCSS.ELA-Literacy.L.K.1.B

I can use the new words that I learn.

You need:

climb	gallop	slither
fly	hop	waddle
float	jump	walk

Finish the sentence using a word you learned. Then draw a picture.

I can

Got it!

OK

Not yet

What's the difference?

Circle what is different between **picture A** and **picture B**.

I can compare two objects using the same tool and describe how they are different.

A **scale** is used to measure weight. When two objects are put on a balance scale, the heavier object will drop down and the lighter object will lift up.

Balance Scale

Circle the animal that is **heavier**.

Cross out the animal that is **lighter**.

Online Extra: To go to this activity, use your smartphone camera, hover over this code, and click on the link. Or go to: **anywhereteacher.com/qr/14162/04.**

Got it! OK Not yet

I can compare two objects using the same tool and describe how they are different.

Circle the object that is **heavier**.

Cross out the object that is **lighter**.

The first one is done for you.

Got it! OK Not yet

CCSS.Math.Content.K.MD.A.2

I can describe the length and weight of an object.

Circle the thing that is **heavier** in each group.

Got it! OK Not yet

I can use words in real life situations to show that I understand what the word means.

Grocery Store Checklist

Look at the picture on the next page.
Check the words below when you find them in the picture.

- [ ] apples
- [ ] bread
- [ ] gallon of milk
- [ ] cheese
- [ ] lettuce
- [ ] food scale
- [ ] bananas
- [ ] popcorn
- [ ] a cashier

Look at the picture on the next page.
Write the answers to the questions.

Is the cashier wearing a **yellow** or a **red** shirt?

What food is in the food scale?

What was your favorite thing on the grocery store list above?

I like

CCSS.ELA-Literacy.L.K.5.C

You need:

Parent Tip:
Have conversations with your child that encourage the use of new vocabulary. Kids learn and make words more concrete through conversations.

Got it!

OK

Not yet

Two of a Kind

You need:

Look at each of the pictures.

Circle the two pictures that are the same.

Got it! OK Not yet

I can be an active learner in nonfiction reading activities.

Cut out the pages below.
Put the pages of the book in order.

In the afternoon,
I eat my lunch.

In the morning,
I eat my breakfast.

In the evening,
I eat my dinner.

MY
MEALS

Parent Tip:
Use your finger when reading. Show top to bottom, left to right.

Got it! OK Not yet

I can find the main idea in a nonfiction text with help.

Read the text and look at the picture. Circle the answers.

What kind of bear is in the picture?

brown bear

black bear

polar bear

What color is the bear?

red

white

gray

Where do these bears live?

America

Arctic

Antarctica

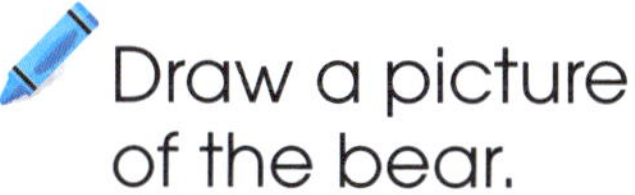

Draw a picture of the bear.

Got it! OK Not yet

You need:

I can read and understand kindergarten books.

Parents:
Please read the book **All About Bears** to your child. Then ask the following questions.

Why did the authors write this book?

To teach us about bears.

To teach us about fishing.

What is a baby bear called?

puppy

cub

Where do polar bears live?

the Arctic

the desert

What colors are panda bears?

brown and white

black and white

How many eyes does a bear have?

2 **3**

Got it!

OK

Not yet

CCSS.ELA-Literacy.RF.K.4

I can explain the connection between two people, events, or ideas in a nonfiction text.

Look at both bears above.

Circle the answers.

Both bears have 2 ears?  

Both bears are brown?  

Both bears have 2 front legs?  

Both bears have black noses?  

Got it! OK Not yet

I can tell reasons and gives details to support an author's ideas in a nonfiction text with help.

 Read the **All About Bears** book.

Answer the questions.

Write what you learned from this book.

I learned

Point to the part of the book you learned this.

CCSS.ELA-Literacy.RI.K.8

I can explain how two books with similar topics are the same and different.

You need:

Find the books **All About Bears** and **Underwater**.

Parent Tip:
When you read books with your child, stop and ask them questions about the book.

Read both books.

Circle the answers.

Are both books about bears?  

Are both books about fish?  

Are both books about animals?  

Do both books have animals that swim?  

Write what you want to learn more about.

Got it! OK Not yet

I can describe the length and weight of an object.

Circle the things that hold **more**.
The first one is done for you.

Got it! OK Not yet

CCSS.Math.Content.K.MD.A.1

I can describe the length and weight of an object.

You need:

Circle the things that hold **less**.
The first one is done for you.

Got it! OK Not yet

You need:

I can use common beginnings to help me decide what a new word means.

Add **un** to the beginning of a word and it means the opposite. Draw a line to match the picture to the statement.

She is **un**happy

She is happy.

His shoe is **un**tied.

His shoe is tied.

Got it! OK Not yet

CCSS.ELA-Literacy.L.K.4.B

I can use common endings to help me decide what a new word means.

Add a **s** to the end of a word, and it means more than one. Draw a line to match the picture to the statement.

I like dog**s**.

I like my dog.

I see tree**s**.

I see a tree.

Got it! OK Not yet

I can compare two objects using the same tool and describe how they are different.

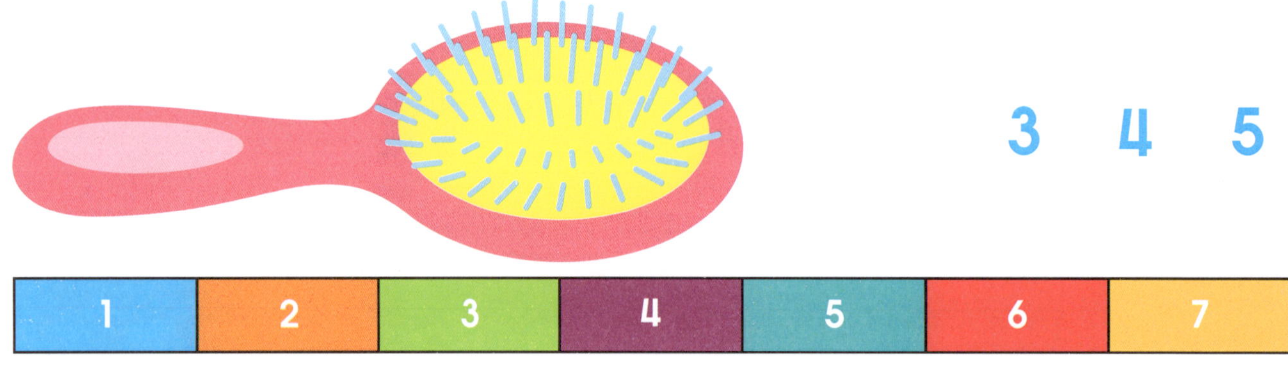

3 4 5

1	2	3	4	5	6	7

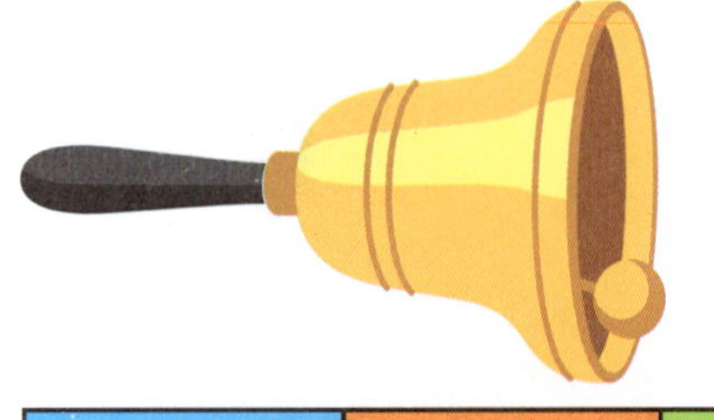

1 2 3

1	2	3	4	5	6	7

4 5 6

1	2	3	4	5	6	7

Measure some things in your room using pennies.
How many pennies long is a pencil?

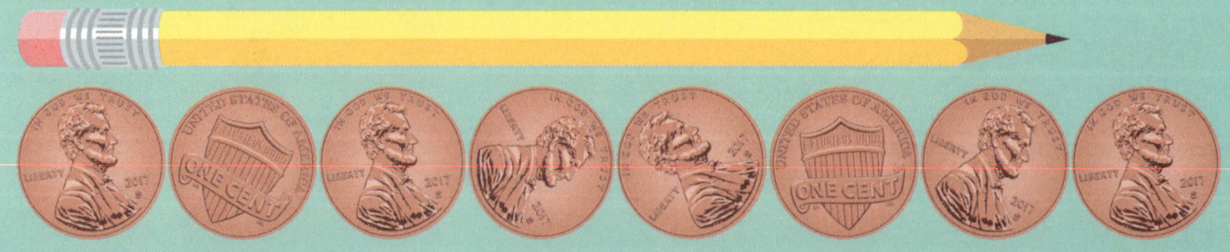

Try using other things to measure like toy blocks, crayons, or your hands and feet. Try using your whole body to measure a hallway or room.

Got it!

OK

Not yet

CCSS.Math.Content.K.MD.A.2

I can compare two objects using the same tool and describe how they are different.

Circle how many ☐ tall each ladder measures.

8	8	8
7	7	7
6	6	6
5	5	5
4	4	4
3	3	3
2	2	2
1	1	1

5 6 7

3 4 5

6 7 8

You need:

I can describe the length and weight of an object.

✓ Check the picture that is **taller**.

✗ Cross out the picture that is **shorter**.

The first one is done for you.

Got it! OK Not yet

CCSS.Math.Content.K.MD.A.1

I can count to 100 by ones and tens.

You need:

Count to **100**.
Write the missing numbers.

1	2	3							10
	12					17			
		23			26				
			34						
				45					
							58		60
			64		66				
71									
								89	
	92								100

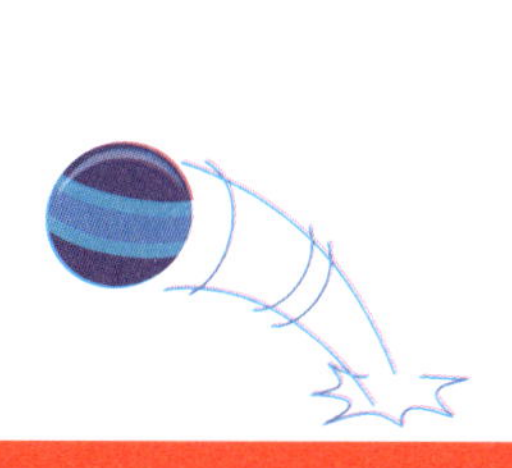

Got it!

OK

Not yet

Let's have some fun!

You need:

Help the robot get to the radio.
Draw a line through the maze from **start** to **finish**.

Got it! OK Not yet